MASON DIXON

FOURTH-GRADE DISASTERS

MASON DIXON

FOURTH-GRADE DISASTERS

CLAUDIA MILLS

ILLUSTRATED BY GUY FRANCIS

Alfred A. Knopf  New York

THIS IS A BORZOI BOOK PUBLISHED BY ALFRED A. KNOPF

Library of Congress Cataloging-in-Publication Data
Mason Dixon : fourth-grade disasters / by Claudia Mills. — Hardcover ed.
p. cm. — (Mason Dixon ; #2)
Summary: Mason Dixon is his usual pessimistic self as he starts fourth grade, dreading joining the school choir and unenthused about his sports-obsessed teacher, who plans for the students to be "making a full-court press on writing."
ISBN 978-0-375-86874-0 (trade) — ISBN 978-0-375-96874-7 (lib. bdg.) —
ISBN 978-0-375-89959-1 (ebook)
[1. Schools—Fiction. 2. Singing—Fiction. 3. Pessimism—Fiction.
4. Friendship—Fiction.] I. Title. II. Title: Fourth-grade disasters.
PZ7.M63963Maf 2011
[Fic]—dc22
2010048721

The text of this book is set in 13.5-point Goudy Old Style.
The illustrations in this book were created using pen and ink.

Printed in the United States of America
November 2011
10 9 8 7 6 5 4 3 2 1

First Edition

To Jennifer Teets

1

"Fourth grade!" said Mason Dixon's mother as she sat on the family-room floor surrounded by bags of school supplies. "Tomorrow is the first day of fourth grade!"

Lying on the floor next to her, Mason tried not to scowl. He must not have succeeded, because she said, "Stop frowning! Fourth grade is wonderful. It will be your best year yet!"

That wasn't saying much. Third grade had meant sitting next to Dunk Davis instead of sitting next to Brody Baxter. Second grade had been Mrs. Prindle, who didn't like boys. First grade had been a broken arm, when Mason fell off the climbing bars. And kindergarten—well, the less said about Mason's biggest kindergarten disaster, the better.

Beside him on the floor, Mason's dog, Dog, snored peacefully. Dog obviously wasn't impressed by the thought of fourth grade. Mason felt a surge of love for Dog, a three-legged golden retriever who had come to live with him two months ago.

"Go sharpen your pencils," Mason's mom said. "I'll put your name on your notebooks. I just love brand-new school supplies, don't you?"

Actually, Mason didn't. The trouble with brand-new school supplies was that they were brand-new *school* supplies.

"I'm so glad you and Brody are in the same class again," she went on.

That was one thing Mason was glad about, too.

"Do you remember that time when Brody was absent in preschool and you went up to another child and said, 'Let's pretend you're Brody'? Your teacher told me that. It was the cutest thing."

Mason felt his scowl deepen. He had already heard the story fifty times. Maybe sixty.

"This year you'll finally get to be in the Plainfield Platters!" his mom said.

The Plainfield Platters was the huge school chorus that practiced before school two mornings a week, open to all fourth and fifth graders. As far as Mason could tell, all fourth and fifth graders were in it. But surely, in the history of Plainfield Elementary, there must have been at least one fourth grader who wasn't.

"Um—I don't like to sing," Mason reminded her, since she had apparently forgotten.

"You have a lovely singing voice!"

Mason couldn't remember any time that she had heard him sing. It wasn't an activity he ever engaged in voluntarily.

In kindergarten, Mason's class had had to sing a song for a school assembly, presumably to show all the bigger kids how adorable they were. The song went,

"I'm a little teapot, short and stout." At the end of the song, when the little teapot got all steamed up and ready to shout, "Tip me over and pour me out!" Mason had tipped himself too far and fallen over, right there in the middle of the front row. The whole school had burst into laughter mingled with cheers, or maybe it had been laughter mingled with jeers.

It had been the worst moment of Mason's entire life. He still dreamed about it sometimes.

"I don't like to sing," Mason repeated. *Especially not in front of the whole school.* "I'm not what you would call a singing person. I don't want to be in the Plainfield Platters."

And I'm not going to be, he added, but only to himself.

"Mason." Now it was her turn to frown. "We're not going to have another year with a negative attitude. Your father and I have been talking about this. If you expect rain, you'll get rain. If you expect sun, you'll get sun."

That might be the single falsest statement Mason had ever heard.

"You expected sun on my birthday," he pointed out, "for my *outdoor* birthday party at Water World. And what did you get?"

"Mason, you know what I mean."

Mason rolled over so that he was lying facedown, his nose squished against the scratchy carpet. In his sleep, Dog must have sensed Mason's presence; Dog's long tail thumped twice. That would be another bad thing about school: leaving Dog all day. Fourth grade wouldn't be so bad if Dog could be there, too.

And fourth grade wouldn't be so bad if there weren't the bizarre expectation that every single fourth grader would stand up on the stage in front of hundreds of people and sing. Oh, and sing while doing the occasional lively dance step as well. In addition to not being a singing person, Mason wasn't a dancing person. Most of all, he wasn't a being-up-onstage-in-front-of-everybody person.

It would be even worse if a big fourth grader fell over while trying to impersonate a tipping and pouring teapot. And Mason hadn't thought his kindergarten calamity was all that amusing in the first place.

"Now go sharpen your pencils," Mason's mother said. "There's nothing like a bunch of freshly sharpened pencils on the first day of school!"

Mason groaned.

"Mason! Go sharpen your pencils!"

Mason went.

Brody came over later that afternoon, to see Mason, of course, but also to see Dog. Mason and Brody shared Dog. Brody couldn't have a dog of his own because his father was desperately allergic to all pets except Brody's goldfish, Albert. In fact, Brody had been the reason Mason got Dog: Dog was supposed to be Brody's dog, but lived next door at Mason's house.

For a while Mason hadn't even liked Dog, hard as that was to believe now. Mason had thought he wasn't a pet person, but he had turned out to be wrong about that. Though not completely wrong. He still wasn't a *pet* person. But he was Dog's person. And Brody was Dog's person, too.

Brody came staggering under the weight of a huge paper sack, which he placed carefully on the floor before swooping down on Dog for a hug. Dog licked

Brody's face, his neck, his hands, any part of Brody that was lickable.

"What's in the bag?" Mason asked Brody once Dog's licking was completed.

"My school supplies! I thought we could compare school supplies."

Mason stared at Brody. Even for Brody, the most enthusiastic person on the planet, this was a bit much.

"Compare school supplies?" Mason repeated in a strangled voice.

"You know, show each other what kind of markers we got, and how many colored pencils we have in our colored-pencil boxes, and if we got anything special. Like, I have a tiny little stapler with miniature staples in it, and my own personal pencil sharpener so I can sharpen pencils right at my desk if I don't want to get up to walk all the way across the room to sharpen a pencil."

"I already sharpened mine," Mason said. "My mother made me."

"I already sharpened mine, too—of course I did—but, Mason, they're not going to stay sharpened all year long. So that's when I'll use my own personal pencil sharpener, shaped like—" Brody's voice broke off. "Guess what it's shaped like!"

Mason couldn't begin to guess. "I give up."

Brody glowed with pleasure at having stumped Mason.

"It's shaped like—a dog! I think it even looks a little bit like Dog."

Brody dug in his sack for the pencil sharpener, pulling out heaps of notebooks with bright, busy covers: pictures of dogs, of cats, of all kinds of fish. Mason's notebooks were plain, solid colors: red, yellow, green. He had wanted them all the same color, brown (to match the brown socks he wore every day), but the store didn't sell brown notebooks. Besides, his mother had said it would be better to have a different color for each subject. She had obviously given a lot of thought to the notebook issue.

"Here it is!"

Brody held out his pencil sharpener, which did look sort of like Dog. The pencil-sharpening hole was in the dog's tail.

"Cool," Mason said, since he had to say something.

"Okay, Mason," Brody announced after a long pause to give Mason time to appreciate the pencil sharpener in its full glory. "Are you ready for a surprise? Because I have a surprise for you!"

Mason generally didn't like surprises. But he couldn't imagine that Brody's surprise would be anything too terrible.

"Sure," he said guardedly.

Brody held out a twin dog-shaped pencil sharpener, which he had been hiding behind his back. "I got one for you, too! Because we're best friends, and co-owners of Dog. Now we'll have matching dog pencil sharpeners!"

Mason returned Brody's grin. It was weird to have a best friend who was so excited about a pencil sharpener, but Mason had nothing against weirdness. Some people even thought that he himself was a tiny bit unusual.

"And wait till you see my eraser!" Brody went on. "You aren't going to believe my eraser!"

This time Mason felt more comfortable venturing a guess. "It's shaped like a dog."

"It is! And guess what, Mason."

"You got one for me, too."

Triumphantly, Brody pulled two matching dog-shaped erasers out of his sack.

"Ta-dah!"

"Wow. Thanks, Brody," Mason said. What else could he say with Brody's face shining like that?

"So it will be like having Dog there with us at school. Fourth grade is going to be great!"

Mason wanted to say that having a dog-shaped pencil sharpener and a dog-shaped eraser was nothing at all like being with a real, live Dog. And he strongly suspected that fourth grade was not going to be great. The best he could hope for was bearable. Being in the Plainfield Platters was not even going to be bearable.

Before Brody could show him any more school supplies, or start talking about how wonderful it was going to be to join the Platters, Mason jumped up and said, "Let's take Dog for a walk."

Brody cast one longing glance back at his sack, but then he jumped up, too. Dog had already dashed into the kitchen and returned with his leash in his mouth.

"This is the last walk we'll ever take with Dog before we're officially fourth graders," Brody said solemnly. "I mean, we were sort of fourth graders once third grade ended, but we were also sort of nothing—

in between, not anything. So this is our last walk as not yet really, truly fourth graders."

Mason knew Brody meant his comment to highlight the grandeur of the moment, but to his ears, it had a doomed sound.

Tomorrow Mason would be a really, truly fourth grader, armed only with a dog-shaped pencil sharpener and a dog-shaped eraser.

He took the leash from Dog with a heavy heart.

Then Dog spied something in Mason's heap of school supplies and pounced on it. Mason couldn't see what it was, but he knew it wasn't something Dog should be eating.

"Dog, drop that!" Mason commanded.

Dog kept on chewing, and then he swallowed it, whatever it was.

Mason looked back at the school supplies to see what was missing.

There was no longer any dog-shaped eraser in the pile.

So tomorrow Mason would be a really, truly fourth grader, armed only with a dog-shaped pencil sharpener.

A really, truly fourth grader who would really, truly be expected to sing and dance in front of everybody.

2

Mason's fourth-grade teacher was a man. Other teachers at Plainfield Elementary had normal names, like Mrs. Prindle and Mrs. Oliphant. Not that those were completely normal names, but at least they were teacher-sounding names. This teacher called himself Coach Joe.

"Good morning, team!" he shouted once everyone had found a desk.

Mason was impressed that Coach Joe was letting kids choose where to sit. Mason chose to sit next to Brody, of course, which meant sitting in the front row, because Brody loved the front row. Tall, skinny Nora Alpers, who had become a friend last summer when they had all been in summer art camp together, sat on Mason's other side. Mason was relieved that Dunk Davis chose a seat in the farthest corner of the back row.

"All right, team! Come on up for a huddle!"

A huddle must be a class meeting. The students gathered on the football-shaped rug in front of Coach Joe's stool.

Coach Joe clearly loved sports. Mason hated sports. So this was a first clue that, despite his getting to sit next to Brody and far away from Dunk, fourth grade was not going to be a good year. Mason sighed, a deep, wrenching sigh that took every molecule of air right out of his lungs. No one seemed to notice, except for Nora, who noticed everything.

Sitting two kids away from Mason in the huddle, Dunk did a few boxing motions in the air, as if to demonstrate his readiness to enter the ring. Dunk's big mean dog, Wolf, had attacked Dog last summer and almost killed him. Or at least might have killed him.

It was unfortunate that Dunk had happened to

walk by Mason's house before school that morning as Mason's mother had him posed outside by the front door, smiling grimly, holding his bulging bag of school supplies, for the first-day-of-school photo that she took every year. Dunk now interrupted his boxing to pretend to snap a picture of Mason and then doubled over laughing.

"Okay, team!" Coach Joe said. "Listen up!"

Coach Joe's hair was cut short in a bristling crew cut. He didn't wear a whistle on a string around his neck, but if he had, it wouldn't have looked out of place.

"Today is the kickoff for fourth grade," Coach Joe said. "If we're going to have a winning season this year, we have to have a winning attitude."

Mason couldn't believe it. First his mother, now his teacher.

Sitting next to Mason in the huddle, Brody gave a huge grin. If anybody had a winning attitude, Brody did. In second grade, Brody had even liked Mrs. Prindle.

"No team," Coach Joe continued, "has ever won the Super Bowl, or the World Series, or the NBA Championship without a winning attitude."

So that made three things Mason wasn't going to win.

The public address system clicked on. It was time for the Pledge of Allegiance, morning announcements, and the singing of the school song.

The students all stood up, crowded together on the football-shaped rug, and turned to face the large flag hanging by the front whiteboard. Mason saw Dunk shove the kid standing next to him; the other kid shoved him back.

Mason joined with the rest of the class in saying the pledge. He half listened to the announcements. The school lunch today was chicken nuggets. Mason was glad he had brought a peanut butter and jelly sandwich from home. Then again, he always brought the same lunch from home: a peanut butter and jelly sandwich, a small apple, and four Fig Newtons.

Then Mason heard the principal say, "The Plainfield Platters will begin practice next week before school on Tuesday and Friday mornings, starting this coming Tuesday."

It was Thursday now—for some reason, a new school year always started on a Thursday—so Tuesday was five days away.

"The Platters are open to all fourth and fifth graders who love to sing."

That left out Mason.

When the announcements came to an end, the tape-recorded piano music for the school song, "Puff the Plainfield Dragon," started to play. Brody bellowed the song at the top of his lungs. Nora, Mason observed, was barely singing at all. Dunk punctuated the song with jabs to the shoulder of the boy he had been shoving before; the boy jabbed back. Coach Joe, busy singing himself, didn't seem to notice, but then, without missing a word of the song, he moved over toward Dunk, and suddenly Dunk was standing somewhere else.

During the song, Mason opened his mouth partway so it wouldn't be too obvious that no sound was coming out of his body. Mason wasn't about to sing in front of other people, even if no one else was looking at him because they were all too busy singing themselves.

"Puff is loved by everyone, because he is so cool!" the other students sang. "Every day we shout hooray that Puff lives at our school!"

Ha! The only dragon that lived at Plainfield

Elementary was a faded, oversized stuffed animal that sat in the display case by the front office. Somebody's mother had bought him for the school a million years ago to be the school mascot, and the music teacher had written new words to "Puff the Magic Dragon" in honor of this new Puff. But nobody loved Puff or thought he was cool, as far as Mason could tell. Well, Brody probably did.

"Go, team!" Coach Joe called out once the song had ended.

"Go, team!" everybody shouted back.

Everybody except for Mason.

That afternoon, Coach Joe called the class into a second huddle. In Mason's opinion, two huddles in one day was excessive.

"This year," Coach Joe said, "we are going to be doing a lot of writing in our class. We are going to be making a full-court press on writing."

Mason didn't know what a full-court press was, but it had to have something to do with sports. It sounded as if it would require a lot of work and effort.

Most of the girls looked excited, except for Nora. That didn't necessarily mean that Nora didn't like writing; it just took a lot to make Nora look excited.

Most of the boys looked pained, except for Brody. Mason knew that he himself must look pained, too. He could feel the misery of a full-court press on writing radiating out from the core of his being. The misery had probably reached his face by now.

A full-court press on writing was another clue that this was not going to be a good year.

"Stories!" Coach Joe said. "Autobiographies! Poetry!"

At the word "poetry," Dunk gave a groan loud enough that Coach Joe could hear it.

"Winning attitude, team!" Coach Joe reminded them. "Let's try that again. Poetry!" He pumped his fist into the air.

A few kids feebly pumped their fists into the air in response.

"Let's try that *again*. Poetry!"

This time the whole class went along, except for Mason. Nora's fist didn't go up very high. But it went up higher than Mason's. Mason didn't want to make Coach Joe mad, but he wasn't the type of person who pumped his fist into the air, any more than he was the kind of person who sang in front of other people. He just wasn't.

Coach Joe continued his pep talk.

"Today we're going to start on our first writing assignment for the school year. Are you ready, team?"

"Ready!" the class chanted back. Mason moved his lips, but he didn't actually say the word out loud.

"All right! A story starts with a character. A character can be a girl, or boy, or a grown-up person, but it doesn't have to be a person at all. Who else could be a character?"

Brody's hand shot up. Some kids didn't like Brody because he was always so eager and enthusiastic, but Mason knew that Brody couldn't help being that way. If Brody tried to keep the answer inside, he'd explode.

"Brody?"

"An animal!"

"Great! A character can be an animal. What kind of animal?"

"A kangaroo!"

"Great! Other animals?"

Various kids suggested a dog, a cat, a saber-toothed tiger, a mongoose, and a butterfly.

"Great!" Coach Joe said to each one.

Mason didn't think having a dog or a cat as a character counted as a great idea. Those were ordinary ideas.

"Let's open this up some more," Coach Joe said. "Your character doesn't have to be an animal, either. What else could it be? Let's get some ideas from way out in left field."

"A flower," one girl suggested.

"Great!"

"A toaster," a boy called out.

"Great!"

Now the ideas came thick and fast: a baseball, a skateboard, a cell phone, a million-dollar bill.

Nora raised her hand. "There's no such thing as a million-dollar bill," she pointed out.

"This is a *story*," Coach Joe said. "In a story, we can have a million-dollar bill if we want."

Nora looked as if she wanted to disagree, but she let it drop.

"A toilet!" Dunk shouted.

Everyone laughed. Even Mason laughed. Coach Joe laughed, too.

"All right!" he said then. "I want you to pick an

inanimate object—that means something that isn't alive, not a plant, not an animal, not a person—and write a story about it. At least three pages long for your first draft."

Mason didn't like how Coach Joe said "first draft." That made it sound as if there would be a second draft, too.

Back at his desk, Mason gripped his pencil and stared down at a blank piece of paper. Maybe he could write about a pencil that didn't want to write a story. He could write about a blank piece of paper that didn't want to have a story written on it.

If only the story could be about a person instead of a thing. Then he could write about a fourth-grade boy who didn't want to be in fourth grade. Or about a fourth-grade boy who didn't want to be in the Plainfield Platters, but whose parents were probably going to make him be in the Plainfield Platters.

Mason kept thinking. During concerts, somebody's father accompanied the Platters on an old upright piano. The piano could be the character. Maybe the piano hated playing for the Plainfield Platters. If Mason were a piano, he would hate that, too.

The piano could go on strike and refuse to play.

The piano could wait until the night of the first big concert and *then* refuse to play.

In spite of himself, Mason felt a stirring of interest in his idea. It was, he had to admit, a truly excellent idea.

Mason could guess what Nora would say at this point: *A piano can't refuse to play. A piano has to play whether it wants to or not.*

He could guess what Coach Joe would say in reply: *This is a* story. *In a story, anything can happen.*

In a story, a made-up piano could refuse to be in the Plainfield Platters.

Maybe in real life, a real, live boy could refuse, too.

3

On Saturday morning, Mason awoke to Dog's long, feathery tail brushing across his face. Dog didn't like it if Mason slept too late. Dog wanted both of them to be up and out, making plans for walks to take and sticks to throw and things to chew.

Lately, Dog had been doing too much chewing of things he wasn't supposed to chew. It had been so hot during the last couple of weeks before school started that Mason hadn't been outside playing fetch often enough with Dog; that made Dog look around for other things to put in his mouth. Or at least that's what Mason's father said.

Right now, as if to prove Mason's father's point, Dog was gnawing the arm off of Mason's hand-knit stuffed monkey. Mason's mother edited an online

knitting newsletter, and their house was full of odd hand-knit objects. Mason himself didn't think it mattered if there were one fewer of them, but he knew his mother would be sad if Dog destroyed something it had taken her hours and hours to make.

"Stop it, Dog," Mason said.

He grabbed the monkey from Dog and threw it across the room.

That was the wrong thing to do. Dog leaped off the bed, sprang after it, and brought it back in his mouth for Mason to throw again.

"Oh, Dog."

Mason forced himself out from under his covers and put the poor monkey on a high shelf in his closet. He had never really liked having it on his bed, anyway. Mason liked to keep his room, and his life, simple and uncomplicated.

Unfortunately, there was nothing uncomplicated about having to break the news to his parents that he was going to be the first fourth grader in the history of Plainfield Elementary not to be in the Plainfield Platters. If he told them today, he'd get it over with. But then they'd have an entire weekend to try to talk him out of it. Still, maybe it would be good to give them a few days to get used to the idea before the first practice on Tuesday, the practice that Mason was planning on not attending.

He found them both in the kitchen, eating quiche and croissants and sipping coffee.

"Bonjour, Mason!" his mother greeted him. She was obviously in a French mood.

Mason poured himself a bowl of plain Cheerios with milk. He was in a plain-Cheerios mood. He was always in a plain-Cheerios mood for breakfast.

"Do you and Brody have any plans for today?" his mother asked.

Mason shook his head. "Brody is doing something with Sheng."

Sheng was Brody's second-best friend. Brody had a third-best friend, too: Julio. And a fourth-best friend: Alastair. And a fifth-best friend: Bradley.

Most of the time, Mason didn't mind. He knew he was Brody's first-best friend. It used to get lonely sometimes when Brody did things with his other best friends. But now Mason had Dog, who really tied with Brody as Mason's first-best friend.

"Do you want to call another friend?" his mother asked.

Mason didn't dignify that suggestion with a reply.

"Or we can go downtown to that free outdoor Indonesian gamelan concert," she suggested. "You've never heard Indonesian gamelan, have you, Mason? It's a unique kind of musical ensemble, sort of like an Indonesian orchestra; they play various instruments, mainly gongs. It's very spiritual music. I read that the players have to take off their shoes before they play. What do you think, Dan?"

Mason's father didn't like strange music and exotic food as much as Mason's mother did, but he was always a good sport.

"Sure," he said.

"It'll be perfect, since this is going to be your year of getting involved with music," she said to Mason. "Starting on Tuesday!"

Now was probably as good a time as any to tell her.

"Mom, I don't want to be in the Plainfield Platters."

That didn't sound forceful enough. So he tried again.

"I'm not going to be in the Plainfield Platters."

She exchanged a worried look with his father, a look that suggested that they had already discussed this alarming possibility and decided how to respond.

"Oh, honey," she said. "We know how you feel about trying new things, but it would be so good for you to do it. Your father and I don't want you to miss out on any of the fun of fourth grade."

What exactly was it about fourth grade that was going to be fun?

"And the more you don't want to do something, the more important it is to do it," she added.

That sounded like a strange idea to Mason. Did it mean that the more you *did* want to do something, the more important it was *not* to do it? Wasn't that completely backward?

His mother looked imploringly at his father for his support.

"Don't you think it would be fun to sing in that group?" his father asked, eyes darting back and forth between Mason and Mason's mother.

In his entire life, Mason had never heard his father sing a single note. At Rockies games, Mr. Dixon never joined in for "Take Me Out to the Ball Game" during the seventh-inning stretch. On their occasional Sundays at the Unitarian church, he moved his mouth during the hymns, but no sound ever came out. That was how Mason had learned to lip-synch in the first place.

"No," Mason said. "I don't think it would be fun."

What could he say to make them understand?

"I'm a little teapot?" he reminded them. "Short and stout?"

Mason's mother looked utterly mystified.

"Tip me over? And pour me out?"

Unbelievably, she seemed to have no idea what he was talking about.

"The assembly? In kindergarten?"

Comprehension dawned on her face, immediately followed by renewed bewilderment.

"But, Mason, that was years ago! And something like that could happen to anybody!"

But it hadn't happened to "anybody"; it had happened to him, Mason. And if it *could* happen to anybody—if this kind of thing was a commonplace, everyday occurrence—didn't that just serve to prove Mason's point, that singing in front of people was an inherently risky business?

"We know this is going to be a stretch for you, honey," his mother continued, keeping her voice gentle. "And we're going to be so proud of you for being willing to step outside of your comfort zone."

Luckily, Dog was standing by the back door, looking very much as if he needed to step outside himself.

"Dog needs to go out," Mason said.

"All right, sweetie," his mother said. "We can talk about this more later."

Goody, Mason thought.

The gamelan concert wasn't too bad. Dog came, too. Dog was very good at not barking during concerts. The gamelan players wore silk costumes. One lady sang. It was sad that in a world where so many people wanted to sing, somebody who didn't want to should have to do it, anyway.

That evening, Mason was afraid his mother would want to have another conversation about the Platters, but instead she just read to him and Dog without saying any more about it. Even though Mason was obviously able to read perfectly well to himself, she liked to read him books that she had loved when she was a girl. Although Mason wouldn't have admitted it out loud, he liked it, too.

Right now they were partway through a book called *Ballet Shoes*, about three English girls named Pauline, Petrova, and Posy Fossil who attended a dancing school in London long ago. Pauline loved to act and Posy loved to dance, but Petrova hated all of it. But so far Petrova was doing it anyway, because she needed to be trained for the stage to earn money for her guardian, whom the girls nicknamed Garnie.

Mason supposed he should be glad that he didn't have to prepare for a career as a professional Plainfield Platter. His parents earned their money in other ways: his mother with editing her online knitting newsletter, and his father with his job working downtown for the city—something to do with roads.

He was that much better off, at least, than Petrova Fossil.

On Sunday afternoon, Mason and Dog were over at Brody's. Dog couldn't come inside the house because of Brody's father's allergies, so they were playing together in the dead garden at the edge of Brody's yard, digging a long channel and filling it with water from the hose. It was Brody's idea. This week Brody wanted to be a bridge builder when he grew up, and he needed a river so he could practice building bridges over it. Dog seemed entirely thrilled with the project, rolling in the fresh dirt, dashing in and out of the water from the hose.

Brody sang as he worked. Loudly.

"I've got the joy, joy, joy, joy down in my heart!" Brody sang. Then he shouted out the question: "Where?" And sang the reply: "Down in my heart!"

"No singing," Mason told him.

"Where?" Apparently Brody couldn't stop himself. "Down in my heart!"

"Brody!"

The singing ceased, but Mason knew that Brody was still humming the song silently in his head. Unfortunately, now the song was stuck inside Mason's head as well.

"We *need* to sing," Brody said. "The first Platters practice is Tuesday, remember?"

As if Mason could forget.

"We'll have Plainfield Platters T-shirts!" Brody shoveled harder in his enthusiasm.

Where? Down in my heart!

"And stand on risers!"

Where? Down in my heart!

"And sing!"

"I'm not going to be in the Platters," Mason said.

Brody stopped shoveling. "Of course you are. Everyone is in the Platters. It's the best thing about being in fourth grade."

"For you, maybe."

"For everybody."

"Not for me."

Now Brody looked worried. "How will we walk to school together on Tuesdays and Fridays if you're not in the Platters?" Then Brody's frown lifted, as if

the solution to the problem had become clear. "Your mother will make you be in it."

"No," Mason said. "I already told her, and she said she understood completely and respected my decision."

Brody looked even more worried. Then he burst out laughing. "Liar!"

Mason tried digging deeper with his shovel, but it struck a rock. He and Brody had been digging for half an hour, and so far all they had was a stupid, muddy hole.

"Down in my heart to stay!" Brody sang.

After another half hour, even Brody was tired of digging, though he kept saying that their pathetic, totally lame river was "awesome" and "totally cool." Dog had given up, too, and lay panting in the shade.

They went back over to Mason's house to make themselves root-beer floats, but before Brody could finish his, Brody's mother called on the telephone and told him that he needed to come back home and turn off the hose. Brody got so excited that he forgot to do things sometimes.

Mason's mother came into the kitchen.

"Did you and Brody have fun?" she asked.

Mason nodded. Even digging a pointless hole in the hot sun was sort of fun if he did it with Brody and Dog.

"Did you think any more about the Platters?" she asked then, in a tone obviously intended to seem casual.

When he didn't answer, she went on. "Your father and I talked some more about it, and we've decided that if after giving it a fair try—a fair try, Mason—you really don't want to do it, we're not going to force you. But we think it's important that you give it a fair try."

"What counts as a fair try?" Mason asked. He had tried it out already in his mind and hadn't liked it one bit. Would a fair try be one practice? Two practices? He hoped it wasn't going to be two whole weeks.

"Three months," she said.

Mason felt the color draining from his face.

"Just until the first concert. And then, after that, it's your decision."

After *that*? She might as well have said, *Just try it for fifty years, and after that, it's* your *decision*.

"Okay?" she asked.

What could Mason say?

He shrugged, which he knew she took as a yes, and swallowed melted ice cream from the bottom of his half-finished float. He had the dread, dread, dread, dread down in his heart, down in his heart to stay.

4

On Tuesday morning, at 7:45, Mason and Brody walked in the door of Plainfield Elementary for the first rehearsal of the Plainfield Platters.

Mrs. Morengo, the retired music teacher who had stayed on at Plainfield Elementary to direct the Plainfield Platters, was a tiny woman, hardly taller than Mason. She was the teacher who had written the words to "Puff the Plainfield Dragon." During his first four years at Plainfield Elementary, Mason had watched her conduct Platters concerts, standing onstage in front of the chorus on a wooden box. As she conducted, she leaped about with such energy that there was always the possibility that she would fall off the box. So far, to Mason's knowledge, she never had.

After Mrs. Morengo's words of welcome, the first song of the day was "Puff the Plainfield Dragon."

"Yes, you all know our Puff," she said. "You have been singing about Puff since the first day of kindergarten, yes? But we begin each year with Puff because he inspires us. We are called the Plainfield Platters. But we are really the Plainfield *Dragons*. Hear us roar!"

Mason noticed that the real-life Puff—the stuffed toy—had been taken out of the glass display case and now sat propped up on a chair next to the piano. Puff leaned to one side, as if he were slightly tipsy.

When the students took their places on the risers in the music room, Mason carefully chose a spot at the very end of the second row behind one of his taller classmates. There was no way he was going to stand next to Brody, front row, center. Mr. Griffith, the dad who played the piano for the Platters, began the opening chords of "Puff." Mason bent his knees and slumped his shoulders so that Mrs. Morengo would hardly be able to see him.

Mason Dixon, invisible dragon, the dragon with the silent roar.

He mouthed the words successfully without attracting any notice to himself. Looking toward Mrs. Morengo, out of the corner of his eyes, he could see Brody belting out the tune as if it were opening night on Broadway for *Plainfield Platters: The Musical*. Brody's second-best friend, Sheng, was standing next to Brody, singing with almost as much enthusiasm.

Mason felt a twinge of jealousy that the two of them were having so much fun together. But it was better to share a love of Dog with Brody than a love of Puff the Plainfield Dragon.

Unfortunately, standing next to Mason was Dunk, who had also chosen a hidden spot on the second row. Dunk seemed to have made it his project for the day to shove Mason off the end of the riser. Mason knew that Dunk didn't have anything against him, particularly; it was just Dunk's hobby to shove people.

"Puff is loved by everyone!" Dunk sang, taking two steps toward Mason while bopping in time with the song.

Mason had no choice but to take two steps closer

to the edge of the riser. In the process, he wobbled forward and bumped into the tall girl in front of him, who turned around and gave him a dirty look. Mrs. Morengo's eyes turned briefly in his direction.

"Because he is so cool!" Dunk took another step toward Mason.

Now there were no steps left for Mason to take. He tried to hold his ground, but it was hard to shove back against Dunk while pretending to sing.

"Every day we shout hooray that Puff lives at our school!"

Dunk won the shoving contest: Mason was off the riser, sprawled on the music room carpet. Once again he was a tipped-over teapot, but this time tipped with

considerably more force and falling a considerably greater distance.

Kids near him burst out laughing.

Oh, how comical to see Mason lying on the floor!

Mr. Griffith broke off playing, and Mrs. Morengo's eyes turned Mason's way as he sat rubbing his left knee and elbow. He'd probably be crippled for life, and instead of telling everybody that it was an old football injury, he'd have to say that it was an old Plainfield Platters singing-group injury.

"Boys!" Mrs. Morengo said sternly, as if Mason's landing on the floor had been as much his fault as Dunk's, a deliberate attempt to arouse his classmates' mirth.

He didn't bother to correct her.

"Here," she said, pointing to the spot in the front row on the other side of Brody. "You. What's your name?"

Mason hoped that she was talking to Dunk, but her eyes were plainly fixed on him.

"Mason," he mumbled.

"Mason. Come stand here, so I can keep an eye on you."

Like a doomed man walking to his execution by firing squad, Mason took his place next to Brody. It was small comfort that Brody greeted him with a radiant grin.

"All right," Mrs. Morengo called out. "Let's try this again. Mr. Griffith, take it from the top."

"Puff the Plainfield Dragon!" everybody sang.

Mason could feel Mrs. Morengo's beady eyes boring into him.

Against his will, he sang, too.

During writing time that morning, Mason read over the start of his story, "The Piano That Went on Strike."

> Once upon a time there was a piano named Pedro. Pedro had a big problem. He did not like playing music.

Mason felt Coach Joe looking over his shoulder. "Great start, Mason! Do you want to tell us a little bit more? Why doesn't Pedro the piano like playing music? What *does* Pedro like to do?"

Mason didn't exactly *want* to tell anything more about Pedro's likes and dislikes, but he supposed he could try to come up with something.

As Coach Joe continued on his way around the room, Mason sat thinking.

"Is Pedro out of tune?" It was Nora, who sat next to Mason on the other side from Brody. "Maybe Pedro doesn't like playing music because he needs to be tuned."

Mason didn't reply right away.

"There has to be a reason why he doesn't want to play."

Mason thought this over.

"There's always a reason for everything," Nora said.

"Is there?" Mason asked.

"Of course! Things don't just happen. Like, when an apple falls on the ground, the reason is gravity. Have you ever heard of Sir Isaac Newton?"

Mason hadn't.

"He was the person who first discovered the law of gravity. And a whole bunch of other laws that explain why things happen the way they do. So you need to figure out why Pedro is the way he is."

"Maybe he's shy," Mason suggested.

Pedro just felt stupid having people plunk on his keys, *plink, plink, plink*, playing whatever dumb notes they felt like playing. "Chopsticks." Did any piano really *want* to play "Chopsticks"?

"Then there has to be a reason why he's shy. There's always a reason for everything," Nora repeated.

Maybe Pedro had a bad experience once, making some terrible, embarrassing mistake playing "Chopsticks" in front of everybody. Or maybe Pedro had been shoved so hard during a practice session that he tipped over and crashed against the floor, to the hysterical amusement of all.

"What's your story about?" Mason asked, to change the subject. Coach Joe didn't mind if they talked, so long as they talked quietly about what they were working on.

"A hundred-dollar bill. Since that *is* the biggest bill that gets made."

"What happens to—him? Is it a boy or a girl?"

"It's an it."

"Does it not want anybody to spend it?"

"It doesn't have thoughts or feelings. It's a very realistic hundred-dollar bill. Someone spends it to buy a bicycle, and then the person who gets the hundred-dollar bill uses it to buy a cell phone. I know, it's a boring story. But at least it could really happen. I like stories that could really happen. If Pedro doesn't like to play music, what *does* he like to do?"

Nothing? "He likes to have people put stuff on him, like piles of music. And coffee cups. And he likes when people dust him. Except when they dust his keys—sometimes it tickles."

Nora laughed. Mason laughed, too.

Usually Mason and Brody walked home from school by themselves, except on days when Brody had soccer practice or a playdate with one of his next-best friends. Mason and Brody went to Mason's house because Brody's parents both worked full-time outside the home, while Mason's mom edited her knitting newsletter from her upstairs home office. And this year, Mason and Brody also went to Mason's house because Mason's house had Dog.

On special days, Mason's mom walked over to Plainfield Elementary to meet them. She must have thought today was a special day, because there she was, standing outside the door of their classroom, chatting with some of the other parents.

"So?" she asked eagerly.

Mason knew what the question meant, but he pretended he didn't.

"How was it?"

He could continue to pretend; he could ask, "How was what?" But there was no point in postponing his answer.

"Not good," he said grimly. She might as well know the truth of what she had signed him up for.

"Dunk Davis pushed me off the riser, and I fell, and I think I sprained my elbow and my knee, so I won't be able to be in the Platters anymore."

At the first part of his sentence she had looked concerned, but at the end of the sentence she just reached over and gave his shoulders a comforting squeeze. Mason should have remembered to fake a limp.

"Now, honey, I think you're exaggerating," she said. "Did Mrs. Morengo scold Dunk?"

"No. She scolded *me*."

Her face showed a flicker of concern again, but

then she made a visible effort to summon her own positive attitude. "Mrs. Morengo has never worked with any of you fourth graders before. I'm sure that once she gets to know all of you, she'll realize what kind of boy Dunk is and what kind of boy *you* are."

By "what kind of boy *you* are," did she mean a boy who doesn't like to sing?

As if to salvage the situation, and rekindle her hopes about their upcoming happy year in fourth grade, she turned to Brody. "What about you, Brody, honey? Did you like your first day in the Platters?"

Brody started telling her everything—what songs they were going to learn for the fall concert, when they'd get their T-shirts, ways that parents could sign up to help.

Mason tuned out. Later, when he was all alone with Dog, he'd tell Dog everything. And Dog wouldn't think he was exaggerating. Dog would know that everything he said about his first day in the Plainfield Platters was completely and absolutely true.

5

At Platters practice on Friday morning, Mrs. Morengo clapped her hands to call the students to attention just as Mason claimed his spot in the second row, this time safely on the other end of the riser from Dunk. He assumed that Mrs. Morengo hadn't meant to condemn him to the front-row center spot for the rest of his life.

"Today," she said, "the fifth graders are going to practice in the auditorium with Mr. Griffith. The fourth graders will stay here with me. You are our newest Platters! It is easy for new Platters to feel lost with so many fifth-grade Platters who are so tall! So confident! So today I want to give *special* attention to my *special* fourth-grade Platters."

She beamed at the fourth graders as the fifth

graders followed Mr. Griffith out of the music room. Mason began to feel uneasy.

"I know there are some wonderful fourth-grade voices here in this room," Mrs. Morengo said. "So today I want to hear each and every one of you sing. All by yourself."

Mason wondered if he could fall down in a heap and get sent home, or at least get sent to the health room. But they'd call his mother, and she'd take him to the doctor, and the day would get steadily worse from there.

"Just a few lines of 'Puff,' the song you already know so well."

Mrs. Morengo looked down at her alphabetical list. "Nora Alpers, will you go first?"

The teacher's gaze swept over the rest of the class. "Don't worry, everybody is going to get a turn!"

Nora walked slowly to the front of the room. Mrs. Morengo, who could play the piano just fine when she wasn't hopping around on her conducting box, pounded out the opening chords.

"Puff the Plainfield Dragon," Nora sang. Her voice was clear and steady, her face without expression. Mason wondered what she was thinking as she sang. That dragons were made-up creatures? That not a single word of the song was true?

Second in line, Evan Anderson had a terrible voice. How could anyone live to be a fourth grader at Plainfield Elementary without knowing the tune to "Puff the Plainfield Dragon"? It was a relief, in a way, to have such a terrible voice at the start of the alphabet. That way everyone else could think, *At least I'm not as bad as Evan Anderson*.

Mrs. Morengo didn't say anything critical after Evan finished his verse. She just made a little mark in her notebook, the same way she had done after Nora.

Brody was the fourth to sing, after Emma Averill. Brody belted out "Puff" as if he had a full orchestra behind him and an adoring audience rising to its feet. Brody's voice was decent, but it wasn't his voice you noticed: it was his face, lit up with happiness to be singing about Puff! The Plainfield Dragon!

Even though Mrs. Morengo was trying not to react either positively or negatively to anybody's singing, she did flash Brody a big smile when he finished. It would have been impossible not to.

The rest of the Bs sang, and then the Cs. No one was as awful as Evan or as enthusiastic as Brody.

Mason knew he'd fall asleep that night to the endless repetition of "Puff the Plainfield Dragon." He'd dream about Puff. He'd wake up in the morning to a chorus of birds chirping about Puff. And Pedro the piano had complained about having to play "Chopsticks"!

Nobody was bothering to listen any longer as their classmates sang, for which Mason was grateful. Instead, they talked quietly among themselves, except for Dunk, whose voice bellowed above the others, ignored for now by Mrs. Morengo.

"Mason Dixon," Mrs. Morengo finally called out.

It was Mason's turn.

Like the others before him, he left his spot on the risers and came to stand next to the upright piano.

Hey, Pedro, he thought, but he was too terrified to be funny, even inside his own head.

From over on the risers, he heard Dunk singing the first line of "I'm a Little Teapot," as if the tune had just happened to pop into Dunk's head.

Mason opened his mouth to sing, but instead he started coughing. The strange thing was that he wasn't faking the cough; it just came hacking out of him of its own accord. But Mrs. Morengo would

probably think he was faking, and it would be one more thing she could blame him for.

Now his classmates, once so busily chatting, had fallen silent. He could feel everybody watching in utter silence, listening to Mason Dixon cough.

From over on the risers, he heard an echoing series of coughs from Dunk. The walls of the music room seemed to ring with the sound of coughing.

Mrs. Morengo and Pedro stopped playing.

"Are you all right, Mason?" she asked.

Mason forced himself to nod. "Something must have gotten stuck in my throat," he said.

Something like his tongue.

"All right, let's try it again," she said. "Children, just visit among yourselves," she instructed the rest of the class, as if that could get them to turn off their suddenly fascinated ears.

Pedro played the opening chords of "Puff" once more. Somehow, Mason managed to get his mouth open and sing, without tipping over like a little teapot. He knew he wasn't smiling, but he didn't think he was frowning, either. He tried to look like Nora.

"Every day we shout hooray that Puff lives at our school!"

He had survived and could go back to the risers with the other kids, who had resumed talking once they realized that Mason's second scene of spectacular humiliation this week had come to its conclusion.

"Mason." Mrs. Morengo was apparently talking to him. "Once you got going, that was lovely. Have you ever taken voice lessons?"

Voice lessons!

Mason shook his head, too horrified by the question to speak. In second grade his mother had tried to make him take piano lessons, without success, but even she had not dared to suggest voice lessons.

Smiling, Mrs. Morengo wrote a name and number on a piece of paper and handed it to Mason.

"Give this to your parents—this woman is a wonderful voice teacher. One of her students now sings for the Central City Opera."

Numbly, Mason took the piece of paper and stuck it in his pocket.

Mrs. Morengo gave him another huge smile; his crime of falling off the risers on the first day had apparently been forgiven and forgotten. "Maybe we can coax you into singing a solo for us at one of our concerts!" she said.

Mason meant to shake his head again, but it was frozen motionless on his neck, paralyzed by her words as by the bite of a poisonous serpent.

Or scalding steam from a tipping teapot. Or the fiery breath of a school-mascot dragon.

"Maybe we'll both get solos!" Brody said as they hurried to Coach Joe's class together.

Walking past them, Dunk sang a series of *la-la-las* in a high, quavery, opera-singer voice. Then he tried out a line of "I'm a Little Teapot" in the same exaggerated falsetto.

Brody ignored Dunk. "I think it's cool that you might take voice lessons. We could both take voice lessons! We could have our own singing group and take it on the road. What would be a good name for our group? How about the Singing Dragons? Or the Dragon Kids? Or—is there some way to combine our names? The Mason Brodys. Or the Brody Masons."

"I don't like to sing," Mason said wearily.

"Oh," said Brody. "I forgot."

Right after the Pledge of Allegiance and the morning announcements, Coach Joe called the class into a writing huddle. At least today they didn't have to sing "Puff" as part of the opening exercises. Maybe the principal had heard the distant sounds of the fourth graders' Platters practice wafting down the hall to her office.

"How are your stories coming along?" Coach Joe asked the class.

"Good!" a few kids called out.

Coach Joe beamed. "You guys have really stepped up to the plate on this assignment, I can tell. Any questions? Any problems? Anyone stuck on base and can't get home?"

One girl raised her hand. "Mine's too short. I don't know how to make it long."

"Great question, great question," Coach Joe said. "Here's how you make a story longer. And better."

He stood up and with a bright red marker wrote one word on the dry-erase board behind his stool: CONFLICT.

"Your main character has a problem, correct?" Coach Joe went on. "She solves it right away, end of story. So don't have her solve it right away. Remember the old saying, 'If at first you don't succeed, try,

try, again'? That's good advice for writing our stories. Don't let your character at *first* succeed. Have her try, and fail. Try, and fail. And *then*, try and succeed."

Mason thought about Pedro the piano. Pedro could break one of his strings. Then the piano tuner would come and fix it. Pedro could spill something on his keys. Then the music teacher would clean it. Then Pedro could just refuse to play.

He thought about Mason the boy. Mason started out refusing to join the Platters. Then his mother made him join. Mason hid in the second row and lip-synched. Then Dunk shoved him off the riser, and Mrs. Morengo made him stand in the front row next to Brody. Mason had his hideous coughing spasm during his private singing. Then Mrs. Morengo said he should take voice lessons and have a solo in a concert, which would be like singing all by himself in front of Mrs. Morengo and his classmates but a hundred thousand times worse.

Now Mason could—? Now Mason could what?

He leaned over and whispered to Nora, "Does your hundred-dollar bill have a problem?"

"No," she whispered back. "You can't have a problem unless you have thoughts and feelings. Well, I guess you could *have* a problem, but you wouldn't know you did, so you wouldn't care."

That was one of the many ways Mason was different from a hundred-dollar bill.

Mason knew he had a problem.

And Mason cared.

6

Saturday morning, Mason and Dog left early for a walk. On school days, it was all Mason could do to force himself out of bed, but on weekend mornings he found himself wide awake while his parents were still sleeping. And these days, the instant he was awake, Dog was awake, too.

That was one of the many satisfying things about Dog.

There was no visible activity yet at Brody's house. Mason knew that Brody had a soccer game later that morning and an afternoon playdate with his fourth-best friend, Alastair. Mason's mother had mentioned something at dinner last night about taking Mason to see a Japanese puppet version of *Peter and the Wolf*.

Mason didn't think he could face Japanese puppets after a whole week of being in the Plainfield Platters. He needed an alternative plan, and he knew his mom wouldn't think watching cartoons with Dog counted.

What Mason really needed was a second-best friend of his own.

Dog stopped to pee. Mason never ceased to be impressed at how Dog could balance so easily on his two left legs while lifting his only right leg. This was another of the many satisfying things about Dog.

Mason could probably share one of Brody's other friends, the way they shared Dog. Sometimes Mason did join Brody and Sheng or Julio when they went to a movie, or bowling.

Still, if Mason had to have a second-best friend, the person he liked best, after Brody, was Nora. Nora was sensible. She had good ideas. Once last summer she had even come over to Mason's house and helped Mason and Brody give Dog a bath.

Or, rather, Mason and Brody had helped Nora give Dog a bath.

Or, rather, Brody had helped Nora give Dog a bath.

Should Mason call Nora on the telephone? What

would he say? *Do you want to hang out this afternoon so I won't have to go with my parents to see a Japanese puppet version of* Peter and the Wolf?

Actually, when he tried out the line in his head, it sounded pretty good.

Or he could say: *Do you want to hang out with Dog and me for a while?*

That sounded pretty good, too.

Breakfast was plain Cheerios and milk for Mason, tofu-and-red-pepper scramble for his parents. Mason hadn't given the piece of paper with the voice teacher's name and number to his parents. He had stuck it at the bottom of a pile of papers on his desk in his bedroom. It wasn't as if Mrs. Morengo were going to call to talk to his parents about it.

Or at least he desperately hoped that she wasn't.

After breakfast, Mason took the phone and the Plainfield Elementary directory up to his room. Dog watched him approvingly as he dialed Nora's number.

"Hi, Nora. It's Mason," he said when she answered. "Mason Dixon. From school."

"You're the only Mason Dixon I know," Nora said. "So you didn't have to say 'from school.'"

There was an awkward pause.

"Dog and I were wondering if you wanted to hang out with us this afternoon."

"Sure," Nora said. "Do you want to come to my house? Like, at two o'clock? I can show you my ant farm."

"Sure," Mason said. "Can Dog come, too?"

"Sure."

Mason would never have guessed that finding a second-best friend could be so easy.

"Oh, Mason!" his mother said when he told her his plans for the afternoon. The visible delight on her face was a bit hard to take. He could only imagine how thrilled she would have been if he had told her about the voice teacher. "This will be so good for you! I told you fourth grade was going to be your best year, didn't I?"

"Mom!" Mason said.

He didn't know what she was making such a big fuss about. He was hardly the first boy in the history of the world to go over to a girl's house to see her ant farm.

At two o'clock sharp, Mason knocked on Nora's door. She lived just a few blocks away, so he and Dog had walked there by themselves.

Nora's dad answered the door. Mason had met him before, last summer at art camp. Like Nora, he was tall and thin and serious-looking.

"Nora!" he called upstairs. "Dog is here! And Mason, too."

Nora petted Dog and let him lick her in his friendly way. Then she led them up the stairs to her neat, orderly room. Mason started to feel more relaxed. His own room was also neat and orderly.

On one wall of Nora's room hung a big map of the

night sky: the northern and southern hemispheres with all their constellations. On another wall hung a big chart of some kind.

"The periodic table of the elements," Nora told him. "You know—hydrogen, helium, lithium, beryllium."

Mason didn't know, but he nodded, anyway.

A tall, thin glass rectangle, filled with what looked like tunneled dirt, sat on a low table. From across the room, Mason couldn't see any ants in it. But it had to be Nora's ant farm.

"Yes," Nora said, reading the question in Mason's eyes. "Come meet my ants."

Sure enough, when Mason drew closer, he could see dozens of ants, busily scurrying. Some were digging. Some were carrying things. They all seemed to know what they were doing.

As Mason watched, Nora lifted off the cover, reached in with a stick, and made a hole in one of the tunnel walls, so that dirt tumbled down, blocking the passageway. Almost instantly, the ants leaped into action to repair it.

Mason felt sorry for them. "Wasn't that kind of mean? To make them do all that extra work?"

Nora stared at him. "Work is what ants *do*."

"But do they like doing it?"

Nora replaced the ant farm cover. "It's what they *do*," she repeated. "It's not a question of like or not like."

Mason had to ask her one more thing. "How come you're in the Plainfield Platters when you don't like to sing?"

"What makes you think I don't like to sing?"

"You don't open your mouth very wide when you do it."

Nora laughed. Then, as if to answer Mason's question, she said, "Everybody's in the Platters."

Her eyes fell fondly again on her ant farm; Mason followed her gaze. All the ants were doing their little ant jobs, none of them complaining or refusing to cooperate.

"But everybody doesn't *have* to be in the Platters," Mason said.

Nora thought about that for a moment. "No," she said.

"It's not like gravity, where everything *has* to fall down instead of up," Mason went on.

"No," Nora agreed. "It's more like falling up would be too much trouble."

They both laughed, but the fact remained: being in the Platters was trouble, too.

During Monday morning's writing huddle, Coach Joe asked the class if anybody was ready to read his or her story aloud.

One hand, and only one, shot into the air.

"Brody," Coach Joe said. "Thanks for being willing to share."

Dunk groaned.

"Team," Coach Joe said in a low, pleasant voice that was more effective in enforcing good behavior than Mrs. Prindle's shrill scolding had ever been. "Okay, Brody, let's hear what you have for us."

"My story," Brody announced, "is about a can opener named Clarence."

Brody began to read. "Once upon a time there was a little can opener named Clarence. And once upon a time there was a huge, enormous, gigantic can. The can was filled with sauerkraut." Brody looked up from his paper. "You know, to put on hot dogs. Some people don't like sauerkraut on hot dogs. But I do."

"What happened next?" Coach Joe prompted gently.

"Clarence worked at a hot-dog stand at the baseball stadium. He opened cans during every game. Cans of ketchup, cans of mustard, cans of relish, cans of sauerkraut."

"Ketchup and mustard don't come in cans," Nora whispered to Mason. "They come in jars or bottles."

Brody heard her. "Well, they might come in cans."

"Let's let Brody finish reading," Coach Joe said. "Then we can give him our suggestions and comments at the end."

"I'm almost to the exciting part," Brody said.

"Okay. One day the king and queen came to the baseball game."

Mason knew Nora must want to ask what country this was that had kings and queens, and baseball and hot dogs. He was wondering that himself.

"The king really wanted a hot dog. He had never had a hot dog before, and this was his chance. And he wanted his hot dog with everything on it. So Clarence had to open the huge, enormous, gigantic can of sauerkraut all by himself. While the king was waiting."

Brody paused again to draw out the suspense.

"Have you ever tried to open a really big can with a really little can opener?" he asked the class. "It's hard. It takes forever. Another can opener would have given up. But not Clarence. 'I think I can, I think I can, I think I can,' Clarence said to himself. And the can got opened!"

Brody beamed at his classmates.

"The end?" somebody asked.

"No. Then the king ate the hot dog and liked it so much that he invited Clarence to come live with him and the queen in their palace and be the royal can opener. And he lived happily ever after."

Coach Joe led the class in applause.

"Any comments for Brody? Remember, we always start with something positive."

"It was funny," Sheng said.

"What part was funny?" asked Coach Joe.

"Having him be a can opener. And calling him Clarence. And having a *can* opener say, 'I think I *can*.'"

"Any suggestions for things Brody can think about as he revises his story?"

A girl named Emily raised her hand. "Clarence didn't try and fail, and try and fail, and *then* succeed, the way you said. He just tried and succeeded right away."

"Good point," Coach Joe said. "Brody, do you think there might be some way Clarence could try to open the can and fail the first time?"

Brody thought for a moment. "He could fall off the can."

Everyone laughed.

"Good! I bet he falls off and gets right back on again. That sounds like Clarence, doesn't it, team?"

It sounded like Brody, too.

But what if Clarence the can opener didn't want

to open cans in front of people, the way Pedro the piano didn't want to play in front of people? Then Clarence could fall off the can and lie peacefully on the counter for a nice long while until everyone decided to leave him alone and not make him open any cans ever again.

That was the story Mason would have written, if he had been writing a story about Clarence the can opener.

7

At Platters practice on Tuesday, Mrs. Morengo finished hearing the rest of the fourth graders do their solo singing. Mason wondered if she told any other kids that they should be taking voice lessons, or if he was the only one.

The first half of the fourth-grade alphabet, those who had done their solo singing for her already, joined the fifth graders in the gym with Mr. Griffith, who was teaching them a new song about raindrops.

Mason thought the raindrop song might be the single dumbest song he had ever heard. There were no words at all, no real words, just "Drip, drop, drip, drop." The children were to start off singing quietly and slowly, to sound like the first raindrops falling at the beginning of a summer storm. As the song went along, the drips and drops came faster and faster, louder and louder—a downpour! Some of the fifth graders were assigned to bang cymbals and drums to represent deafening claps of thunder. Then, after the big storm was over, the song ended with just a few scattered voices singing "drip" and "drop." The song ended with one last, final, tiny "drip."

Mason wondered if he would prefer banging the cymbals to singing. He decided that, for all its faults, singing was less risky.

"Drip! Drop!" the Platters sang. "Drip, drip, drip, drip, drop!"

"Drip! Drop!" Mason mouthed. Even mouthing the words, it was easy to get the drips and drops mixed up. But probably it didn't matter very much, either way.

Following the Pledge of Allegiance on Wednesday, the principal herself began reading the morning announcements. This was unusual: after the first week of school, the pledge and announcements were always read by kids from different classes.

Mason had had to read them once, back in second grade. He had stumbled over the words of the pledge, even though they were written in big print on a large sheet of paper. Instead of "republic," he had said "peerublic," and Mrs. Prindle thought he had done it on purpose to be funny. As if! That had been, even for second grade in Mrs. Prindle's class, an unusually terrible day.

"Boys and girls!" Mrs. Miller's voice came over the PA system. "I have some exciting news to share with all of you!"

Mason's ears perked up. Was school going to close early?

"We have just received word that our school, our very own Plainfield Elementary, has been chosen for a wonderful honor. We have been picked as one of only five schools in the entire state of Colorado to be named a Beulah Brighton Belvedere School for the Arts!"

Whatever a Beulah Brighton Belvedere School for the Arts was, she sounded extremely excited about it. Mason started to tune out as she blabbed on about Plainfield's all-school art show, fifth-grade handbell choir that had played last year at the state capitol, and "of course, our beloved Plainfield Platters!"

Mason started thinking about Dog, who was

in trouble for chewing the trunk off his mother's hand-knit elephant pillow. An elephant without a trunk wasn't much of an elephant. Dog had looked ashamed when he was scolded, but Mason didn't know if Dog really understood what he had done that was so terrible. Mason and Brody were going to play extra games of fetch with Dog after school today to see if that would help Dog break his new bad habit.

"I know I'll see all of you at the special celebration concert next Friday!" he heard Mrs. Miller say.

Mason had missed something. Was there going to be a concert *next week*? Were the Platters singing in it? But Mrs. Miller had finished speaking.

He looked over at Brody, who flashed him an excited grin. An excited grin from someone who was always excited wasn't very informative.

As they opened their math books to work on division, Mason whispered to Brody, "What did she say?"

"We're singing! Next week! On TV!"

That couldn't be right—not the part about singing on TV. But it could be true that the very first Platters concert was barely more than a week away.

Was that good news or bad news? Mason's mother had said he had to be in the Platters for three months, until the first concert. Would this count as the first concert, the concert that would free him forever from being in the Platters? Or would he have to stay in the Platters for three months anyway, and sing in not one but two concerts?

He asked her that night at supper. His parents were eating a suspicious-looking Greek casserole made out of eggplant, called moussaka; Mason was eating a grilled cheese sandwich. They had already read the flyer sent home about the great honor awarded to Plainfield Elementary.

"Mom, if the Platters are having a special concert next week, does that mean that my fair try will be over and I can quit?"

She looked so sad at the question that Mason was almost sorry he had asked it. But then again, *she* didn't seem to mind that *he* had the sadness of being pushed off the risers by Dunk, and the sadness of being overcome with a coughing fit during his "Puff" solo, and the sadness of having to pretend to sing a song about dripping and dropping raindrops.

"Oh, honey," she said. "I thought you were starting to like being in the Platters."

What possible reason could she have had for thinking that?

She looked over at Mason's father, who suddenly had his mouth stuffed with an unusually large forkful of moussaka.

"What do you think, Dan? Less than three weeks just doesn't seem very long to me, to be in the Platters."

Well, his mother wasn't *in* the Platters!

"What if the concert is horrible?" Mason demanded.

"Mason, it's not going to be horrible."

Another statement for which she had absolutely no evidence.

"What if it is?"

"How about we'll cross that bridge when we come to it."

Lying under the table, Dog whacked Mason's leg sympathetically with his tail. Mason reached down and rubbed Dog's silky ears.

Didn't his mother mean they'd cross that bridge after Mason had already plunged off it, catapulting into the churning rapids below?

At Platters practice on Friday morning, Mrs. Morengo was flushed with agitation.

"We have one week! To prepare three songs for the concert! One week!"

The whole school would be at the concert. All the parents would be at the concert. A *Plainfield Press* news reporter and photographer would be there. And Channel 9 News. Yes, Brody had been right: the Plainfield Platters, after just one more week of practice, were going to be on TV.

Mason couldn't believe that people would watch them on TV, not if they could change the channel with their remote control. But there were probably thousands of people whose remotes had fallen down between the couch cushions.

"We'll do 'Puff'—thank goodness for 'Puff'! And the raindrop song we've started working on. For the third song, we'll do a patriotic medley, since most of you know those songs already."

Next week, Mrs. Morengo told the students, there would be Platters practice every single morning. At least Mason wasn't the only one who seemed horrified. One fifth grader pretended to stab himself in the stomach. Dunk staggered a few steps and fell down as if dead.

"I know," Mrs. Morengo said with a kindly smile. "It's hard to get up early five mornings in a row. But think how proud you'll all be when we perform on television on Friday night!"

No, not all.

Not Mason Dixon.

The Platters began practicing the raindrop song. Mason remembered hearing about something called Chinese water torture, where people went insane from being forced to listen to the endless sound of a dripping faucet. Chinese water torture had a lot in common with the Platters' raindrop song.

"Drip! Drop! Drip! Drip! Drip!"

Mason tried to finish his Pedro the piano story during writing time that morning. In the story, Pedro had just finished spilling something on himself. Mason made it be Coke. His mother kept telling him how bad soda was for his teeth, not that she ever bought any, but in case he was ever at a party where soda was served. If Coke was bad for teeth, it was probably bad for piano keys. Piano keys looked like the long, yellowish teeth of a piano.

Sitting next to Mason, Nora was reading a thick nonfiction book about how every single machine ever invented in the history of the world worked. She was already done with her story.

"What would you use to clean piano keys?" Mason asked her. "If Coke got spilled on them?"

Nora looked up from her book. "People shouldn't have Coke near a piano."

Mason wondered if he needed to write how Pedro had gotten the Coke in the first place. A piano couldn't very well walk to the fridge, open it, and pour himself a glass of soda. Maybe some badly behaved kid, like Dunk, had left his Coke on Pedro.

"Is it an electric piano or a real piano?" Nora asked. "Because if it's an electric piano, it's probably ruined."

Mason perked up on Pedro's behalf. Could Pedro be electric? But in his heart of hearts, he knew Pedro wasn't electric. He was a regular upright piano, like Mrs. Morengo's.

"Real."

"My mom just wipes our piano keys with a damp cloth. You don't want to get water inside a piano, whatever kind of piano it is. But you shouldn't have Coke near your piano," she said again, severely.

"I don't have a piano. It's Pedro. The piano in my story."

"Oh. Well, good luck cleaning him," Nora said, and went back to her book.

That evening before bed, Mason's mother read him another chapter of *Ballet Shoes*.

Dog liked the story, too; Mason could tell by the way Dog looked attentively at Mason's mother when she read.

Now poor Petrova, in the story, was in a play—and a play by Shakespeare, no less: *A Midsummer Night's Dream*. In one of her scenes, she had only two words to say: "And I." She kept getting them wrong, saying the words too high or too low, like a squeak or a growl.

"Which character is your favorite?" Mason's mother asked when she closed the book for the night.

"Petrova."

"I thought you'd like her best. Not to spoil the story for you or anything, but she ends up doing very well in the play."

"Does she end up liking being in the play?" Mason asked.

His mother hesitated. "Well, no. She never likes the stage the way that Pauline and Posy do. But she does find a way to do the thing that *she* loves: flying airplanes."

Luckily, Mason had already found a way to do the thing that *he* loved, which was sleeping next to Dog. After his mother turned off the lights and left the room, that's what he did.

He dreamed about a flying teapot, spilling Coke on a shy piano.

8

The weekend was pleasant. Brody didn't have any plans with his other friends, so after his soccer game on Saturday morning, he came over to play a good hour of fetch with Mason and Dog.

On Sunday afternoon, Nora joined them. This time she was the one who called Mason, proof that she did indeed want to be his second-best friend, although since Brody was there, too, maybe now she was also Brody's sixth-best friend.

Nora knew a new game to teach Dog. Being a golden retriever, Dog was already an expert at fetch the stick, and also very talented at go get, the game where he had to get Mason's sock, or Brody's hat, or Nora's shoe.

"This game is called the shell game," Nora said.

"But we're going to play it with buckets instead of shells. Or pots and pans. Anything that can cover up a dog biscuit. And we need dog biscuits. You do have dog biscuits, don't you?"

From the kitchen Mason collected a box of dog biscuits. In the garage Brody found three buckets of different sizes. Because Brody spent so much time at Mason's house, he knew where everything was, sometimes even better than Mason.

"Okay," Nora said. "Now line up the buckets, and while Dog isn't looking"—Mason turned Dog's head away and held on to it so he couldn't see the buckets as Brody placed them in a row—"put a dog biscuit under one of them."

Brody did as Nora instructed.

"Now let Dog try to find which bucket has the dog treat."

It took a little while for Dog to understand the game. Mason had to lead him over to each bucket in turn and allow him to sniff at it. But once Dog caught on, he ran from bucket to bucket, his nose aquiver, yelping with triumph when he found the right one, and nosing it aside to pounce on his reward.

They played until the box of dog biscuits was

empty. It had been three-quarters empty when they started, so Mason didn't feel guilty for overfeeding Dog. Once he'd had a goldfish, named Goldfish, who had died from overfeeding, so Mason was careful never to feed Dog too much.

"Now what?" Mason asked Nora and Brody.

"We could go to my house and work on my bridge," Brody suggested.

So they did. Mason wouldn't have pointed this out, but Nora was a much better bridge builder than Brody, even though Brody was the one who wanted to be a professional bridge builder when he grew up. Nora's bridge had rock supports underneath it and stone steps leading up to it.

Even Brody noticed how much better Nora's bridge was.

"Maybe you should be a famous bridge builder, and I'll be a famous something else," Brody said. "I'll be a famous singer!"

In preparation for his new career, he began singing the Platters raindrop song, starting in the middle, heading toward the exciting part.

"Drip, drop, drop, drop, *drip, drip, DRIP!*"

Dog barked along with Brody's singing. For a dog who was terrified of thunder, he did a pretty good thunder imitation. Maybe Mrs. Morengo would let Dog be in the concert instead of Mason.

Nora said, "I have an idea."

Brody's rainstorm was over, the last little drop fallen. The mighty thundering Dog lay panting on the grass.

"What is it?" Mason asked. Nora's ideas didn't make him nervous. Nora always had good ideas.

"You don't want to sing in the concert, right?"

Mason didn't remember ever telling Nora that. Maybe it was obvious, at least to someone as observant as Nora.

"Tell Mrs. Morengo you want to flash the lights

on and off to be like lightning. And you can turn the audience lights off at the start of the concert and turn them back on at the end. Tell her you'll be the stage crew. That way you're *in* the concert but *not* in the concert."

"Nora," Mason said, "how did you get to be so smart?"

Nora shrugged. "It's just how I am."

When Nora said it, it wasn't bragging.

It was true.

Then came Monday, with Platters practice at 7:45, because this was the week of the concert, the week of having Platters practice every single day.

Mrs. Morengo looked flustered that morning.

"Are we starting with 'Puff'?" a fourth grader asked her.

"No!" Mrs. Morengo almost barked. "We have *five* days! To learn *two* new songs! To perform on television! We don't have time for 'Puff'!"

Mason noticed that stuffed-dragon Puff had completely tipped over and was lying halfway off the chair, with his feet on the chair and his head upside down on the music room floor.

Brody apparently saw, too. He darted out of his place in the front row and set Puff back upright on his chair again, frowning as he studied Puff's turned-up tail.

"Mrs. Morengo?" Brody asked. "Did you know that Puff's tail is ripped in a couple of places, and his stuffing is starting to come out? Should we get him fixed before the concert? In case the television cameras zoom in on him for a close-up?"

Mrs. Morengo clutched her head with her hands.

"Brody, right now Puff is the least of my problems."

"Mason's mom can fix him," Brody persisted. "She's a famous knitter, and knitting is sort of like sewing, so Mason and I could take him to Mason's house after school today, and she can probably sew him."

Mason's stomach clenched. The last thing he needed was for Mrs. Morengo to be talking to his mother about repairs to Puff—or about voice lessons.

Mrs. Morengo forced a smile. "All right, Brody, that would be very helpful. We want Puff to look his best for our concert. But now, Platters, we cannot focus any more on Puff. You need to be raindrops. Mr. Griffith?"

Mr. Griffith played the first raindrop note on [illegible] piano. The chorus of drips and drops began.

Mason didn't think he was going to be able to ask Mrs. Morengo today about being the lightning guy and stage crew for the concert. He'd have to wait until she was in a better mood, not so stressed. But was she going to be in a better, not-so-stressed mood between now and Friday?

During the class writing huddle that day, to Mason's surprise, Dunk volunteered to read his story.

"Is it about a toilet?" one kid asked.

Everyone laughed, including Coach Joe. Mason wondered if Coach Joe was secretly nervous. A story about a toilet was bound to have words in it that somebody's parents might not like. And then the parents might complain to the principal, and Coach Joe might get fired.

"Does someone poop in it?" another kid called out.

Before Dunk could answer, Coach Joe said, "Team, I think it's cool for you to write about whatever character you choose, and we're going to listen to everybody's story with attention and respect. If Dunk's story is about a toilet, we're going to help Dunk make sure that he has created an *interesting* toilet with a *well-developed* problem. We're not going to judge Dunk's story one way or another just because of his choice of a character. It's what he *does* with it that matters. Okay?"

The class settled down.

"All right, Dunk, go ahead. Introduce us to your main character."

"It's not a toilet," Dunk said sadly.

Some of the boys groaned in disappointment.

"My dad wouldn't let me write about a toilet. So my story is about a football. His name is Footie."

Dunk began to read. Footie the football played in a football game. The center snapped him to the quarterback, who passed him to a wide receiver, who ran down with him to the end zone, and Footie won the game.

"And Footie was very happy," Dunk concluded.

Dunk's story was very short, as Sheng pointed out.

"I like stories that are short," Dunk said. "Then nobody gets bored reading them."

"Yeah, but some stories are too short," Sheng shot

back. "I mean, you could have just said: 'Footie was a football. Someone kicked him over the goalposts. He won the game. The end.' "

"What's wrong with that?" Dunk demanded.

"Well, it isn't very much of a story."

"Okay, boys," Coach Joe said. "Dunk, I think Sheng just means that readers would like to hear more about Footie's adventures, right?"

Sheng gave a half nod. Mason knew that Sheng really meant he thought Dunk's story was bad. Which it was.

"My dad should have let me write about the toilet," Dunk muttered.

Mason himself didn't want to hear very much about a toilet's adventures. Then again, he didn't want to hear very much about Footie the football's adventures, either.

After school, Mason went with Brody to the music room to pick up Puff and bring him home for mending. Puff wasn't there.

"He's probably back in his display case," Brody figured out. "That's where Puff lives. He just comes to

Platters practice to give us moral support, especially now that we have our big televised concert coming up."

Sure enough, that's where they found him. Mason noticed that Brody was right: Puff's tail did badly need to be sewed.

The case was locked.

"Now what do we do?" Mason asked.

Going home to Dog and forgetting all about Puff was one good option.

"We'll ask the secretary in the office if she can open the case for us," Brody said.

Mason was glad that Brody did all the talking. "Mrs. Morengo said we could take Puff home so that Mason's mom can mend him before the concert," Brody told Mrs. Boyer, who sat at a desk behind an open glass window in the front hallway by the principal's office.

Mrs. Boyer hesitated; then she said, "I suppose that's all right."

After all, it would be hard for anyone to look less like a dragon-stealing criminal than Brody Baxter.

The principal came up behind her.

"Mrs. Miller, is it all right if these boys take

Puff home for mending?" Mrs. Boyer asked. "Mrs. Morengo wants Puff to look his best for the concert on Friday."

That wasn't quite right. Brody was the one who wanted Puff to look his best for the concert.

Mrs. Miller smiled at Brody the way grown-ups always did.

"That's fine. Just get him back to school by Thursday morning. And make sure you take good care of him. Did you know that Puff is almost twenty years old? For twenty years, Plainfield students have loved Puff just the way you do."

The principal herself unlocked the display case and placed Puff in Brody's outstretched arms. Puff was almost as big as Brody.

Mason could tell that Brody was overwhelmed that such an enormous honor had been bestowed upon him. Compared to the honor of carrying home Puff the Plainfield Dragon, being named a Beulah Brighton Belvedere School for the Arts was nothing.

"You don't have far to go, do you, boys?" Mrs. Miller asked, her face darkening with concern.

"Just five blocks," Brody piped up from behind Puff's head.

Then the two boys, and one dragon, headed out the front door of Plainfield Elementary School.

Mason hoped they wouldn't run into Dunk. Dunk might try to grab Puff (singing a few more loud *la-la-las* in the process), and there might be a scuffle, and Puff might fall into a mud puddle or get ripped even worse than he already was.

Luckily, Dunk was nowhere in sight. Brody carried Puff proudly down the street, Mason bringing up the rear in their royal procession.

Dog came bounding to the door to greet them.

"Down, Dog!" Mason commanded as Dog tried to jump up on Brody to get a closer look at a possible new dragon friend.

Dog definitely seemed interested in Puff.

As interested as he had been in the stuffed monkey that no longer had an arm and the stuffed elephant that no longer had a trunk.

9

Mason's mother examined Puff with care once Dog was lying obediently on the floor, his head on his paw.

"It will be easy to fix him," she said. "What a good idea to bring him here, Brody! I've been hoping for a chance to help with the Platters this year, and what better way than to do some sewing surgery on Puff himself?"

After their snack—three Fig Newtons and milk—Mason and Brody took Dog for a long walk to give Mason's mother a chance to sew on Puff in peace.

"I have a bad feeling about this," Mason said as they stopped in front of a neighbor's tree to let Dog pee.

"A bad feeling about what?" Brody asked.

"Bringing Puff home. With Dog. You know how Dog is these days about chewing."

"Mason!" Brody sounded shocked. "Dog wouldn't chew *Puff*!"

Why, exactly, did Brody think that?

"Give Dog some credit!" Brody almost sounded cross at this aspersion on Dog's character. He stooped and gave Dog an extra-big, defensive hug when Dog finished peeing. "You wouldn't chew Puff, would you, boy?" he asked him seriously.

Dog barked his answer.

"See?" Brody said. He clearly took Dog's bark to mean, *Of course not, dear Brody. How could Mason possibly think I would do such a thing?*

Mason hoped Brody was right. He was also going to make sure that Puff was locked up tight whenever his mother wasn't working on him. He hoped she finished very soon. And he hoped she wasn't going to talk to Mrs. Morengo while she was working on Puff—about voice lessons or anything else.

Mason felt sick inside from hoping.

During Platters practice on Tuesday, Mrs. Morengo spent half the time on rain dripping and dropping, and half on the patriotic medley, which was called "America!" It was a smushed-together mixture of "My Country, 'Tis of Thee," "America the Beautiful," and "God Bless America." The important thing for this song, Mrs. Morengo told the Platters, was to look as patriotic as possible.

"Stand up tall!"

The Platters, including Mason, stood up taller.

"Shoulders back!"

The Platters, including Mason, pulled their shoulders back.

"Tummies in!"

Mason wondered what was especially patriotic about a tucked-in tummy, but he tucked his in.

"Now gaze into the distance. You see a sweet land of liberty. You see spacious skies and amber waves of grain. You see the ocean, white with foam!"

Mrs. Morengo must have decided that her singers looked sufficiently patriotic, because she signaled to Mr. Griffith to begin playing.

"Sing!" she commanded majestically.

The Platters sang, except for one lip-synching Platter on the end of the second row.

As he stood in patriotic pose, not singing, Mason

thought about Puff. His mother had finished mending Puff yesterday evening, but she decided that Puff needed to be cleaned so that he would be returned to school almost a brand-new dragon. Mason had reminded her three times that morning to be sure to leave Puff in her office with the door shut all the way.

The only difficult part about the "America!" number was that eight students in the front row had to hold pieces of cardboard behind their backs, seven printed with the letters of A-M-E-R-I-C-A and one with the exclamation point. At a signal from Mrs. Morengo, the students were to produce their letters, in order, to spell out the word and trigger the crowd's applause.

On the first try, two students held their letters upside down. Mason couldn't see their mistake, but he heard Mrs. Morengo's cry of anguish.

"M! Exclamation point!"

She showed those two students exactly how to hold their cardboard letters, and they tried it again. But this time it was the R that was upside down.

Mrs. Morengo looked ready to cry. Evidently she was picturing thousands—tens of thousands?—of Plainfieldians, perhaps even people from all over the

state of Colorado, watching Channel 9 News and seeing that upside-down R.

Mason was gladder than ever that he wasn't standing in the front row. Brody, holding the I, could be counted on, of course. Brody would never hold the fifth letter in "America!" the wrong way. Though come to think of it, the I would look the same either way.

Mason wasn't about to make any suggestions. He had to conserve his suggestion-making energy for asking Mrs. Morengo whether he could flash the lights during the raindrop song.

As soon as rehearsal was over, he forced himself to

approach her while she was gathering the letter cards from the fourth graders in the front row.

"Mrs. Morengo?"

She didn't seem to hear him, so he tried again, more loudly.

"Mrs. Morengo? I was wondering—"

"T-shirts!" she shouted suddenly, as if alerting the students to T-shirt-shaped missiles about to tear through the classroom wall. Mason half expected the Platters to drop to the floor and cover their heads with folded arms.

"I forgot the T-shirts! Fourth graders, I need you to stay a little longer."

Handing out the shirts took long enough that the second bell was ringing as everyone hurried to Coach Joe's class, all wearing their green Plainfield Platters T-shirts, with Puff's face in a big yellow circle on the front. Kids had grabbed the shirts in a great frenzy, without checking whether they ended up with small, medium, or large.

Brody, the shortest boy in the class, had on a large T-shirt that hung to his knees like a dress.

Mason, one of the tallest boys in the class, had

on a small T-shirt that made him feel like a sausage stuffed into its casing. A big, fat sausage stuffed into a bright green casing.

He glanced over at Nora. As he would have expected, her T-shirt fit just right.

Mason and Brody took one look at each other and began peeling off their T-shirts to trade. Mason heard the seams of his rip as he yanked it over his head.

More mending for his mom to do. Mason hoped that by the time he got home from school, Puff would be mended and cleaned and ready to go back to his nice, safe display case at school tomorrow.

There was a quiz in math: multiplication and division, mainly a review from third grade. Mason was pretty good in math, so he thought he got most of the answers right. In social studies, they were going to spend all year studying the first half of American history, starting with the Native Americans. Coach Joe told the class that next month they would have an Indian powwow, complete with costumes and war paint.

Mason hated costumes; he despised Halloween. Although he had never yet worn any war paint in his almost ten years of life, he strongly suspected that he would not enjoy war paint, either. Maybe he could be absent that day.

But, as his mother would say, he'd cross the war-paint bridge when he came to it. Far more terrifying bridges lay closer at hand.

During writing time, Mason finished the scene with the piano cleaner who came to school to scrub the spilled Coke from Pedro's sticky keys. Then he started writing the climax scene: Pedro's stunning refusal to play on the night of the big concert.

> Then it was the night of the concert! The gym was filled with hundreds of people. The people could hardly wait for the concert to begin.
>
> A TV crew was there, too. They set up a big camera, the biggest camera Pedro had ever seen. Soon thousands of people from all around the state of Colorado would be watching Pedro play.

Maybe even from all around the country.
Maybe even from all around the world.

Mason put down his pencil. His fingers were sweaty from gripping it so tightly. He didn't think he could stand writing any more today.

He heard Dunk's voice. "My story's long now!" Dunk was saying to Sheng, who sat next to him.

Dunk picked up his story and waved it in Sheng's face. Even from where he was sitting, Mason could see that Dunk had three sheets of paper entirely covered with his messy writing.

"So?" Sheng asked.

"So, you can't say it's too short anymore."

Sheng shrugged, as if to say that he hadn't been lying awake at night worrying about the length of Dunk's story. Sheng's own story was about a B-52 bomber that won World War III practically all by itself; he had shared part of it with the class last week.

"Do you want to hear it?" Dunk asked Sheng.

"Not really."

Despite this lack of encouragement, Dunk began to read:

"The Tigers won the toss and chose to receive, but their first possession resulted in a punt of Footie after going three and out. The Lions took the field for the first time, with Footie at their own twenty-seven-yard line. The Lions put together a drive that went fifty-three yards and resulted in a thirty-eight-yard field goal by the kicker who kicked Footie."

Sheng cut Dunk off before he could read any more. "So it's long. Long isn't the same thing as good."

But Dunk's story *was* good—maybe not good as a story, but good as a description of a football game.

"Wow, Dunk," Brody said. "You should be a sportswriter for the *Plainfield Press*."

Dunk beamed at Brody's praise.

Mason looked over at Nora. He couldn't tell what she was thinking. But he could tell that she was thinking something.

After school, Brody had soccer practice with Julio; Julio's dad drove them. So Mason walked home alone.

If Nora was going to be a famous scientist or bridge builder, and Brody was going to be a famous bridge builder or singer, and even Dunk was going to be a famous sportswriter, what was Mason going to be?

Maybe he didn't have to be a famous anything. His own parents weren't famous, but they were happy, most of the time, give or take their worries about Mason's attitude toward being in the Plainfield Platters.

Dog wasn't a champion dog, entering national dog shows on TV, but he was still the best dog in the whole world. His full name was even D.O.G.—Dog of Greatness.

Mason quickened his steps as he turned up the front walk to his house, where Dog would be waiting. He felt sorry for people who didn't have a dog to come home to. He felt sorry for people who didn't have *this* Dog to come home to.

He pushed open the door and, sure enough, Dog came racing down the stairs to greet him, with something hanging from his mouth that looked like a green plush dragon tail.

It *was* a green plush dragon tail.

"Oh, Dog!" Mason wailed. "How *could* you?"

10

"Mom!" Mason bellowed from the front hallway. "Mom!"

She came running from the backyard, where she had been hanging out laundry on the clothesline.

Mason was trying to get Dog to drop Puff's tail without making Dog think this was a game of tug-of-war, otherwise known as "let's see if we can completely destroy Plainfield Elementary School's twenty-year-old mascot."

"Drop it, Dog," Mason said in his authoritative fetch-game voice. But for some reason, Dog didn't feel like dropping Puff's tail. He seemed to know this was a prize far grander than a tossed stick or tennis ball.

Finally, Mason's mother disappeared into the kitchen and returned with a can opener and a can of Dog's favorite brand of dog food. Dog dropped Puff's tail at Mason's feet and sprang toward his reward.

Mason glared at his mother. "Mom, I told you to keep Puff where Dog couldn't get at him!"

If Brody had been there, Mason would have glared at Brody, too: *Oh, Dog would never chew PUFF!*

Mason's mother had the grace to look guilt-stricken. "Mason, honey, I did keep the door of my office shut all day. But then the doorbell rang, and it was the FedEx truck, and I ran down to get my package, and then I remembered the laundry that needed to come out of the washer. . . ."

Her voice trailed off.

"Well," she said, "I guess we should go see what's left of Puff."

Mason trailed behind her as she slowly climbed the stairs. There was no point in running now.

On the floor in her office lay half of Puff. Unfortunately, it was the bottom half, minus Puff's tail. Puff's tail was in good enough condition, even after the tug-of-war, that Mason's mother could have sewed it back on. But apparently Dog had eaten Puff's head.

Doggy footsteps came padding up the stairs. Dog, contented now from a full can of dog food plus one stuffed dragon head, looked ready to lie down on the floor for an after-meal siesta.

"Dog!" Mason yelled.

He took Dog by the collar and dragged him over to where Puff's headless, tailless body lay on the carpet. "Look what you did!"

Dog gave a whimper of shame and dropped his head on his paw, gazing up at Mason with pleading, bewildered eyes: *I didn't know! I would never do anything to make my boy look at me that way!*

Mason couldn't stay angry at Dog. "Oh, Dog," Mason said sadly, and stooped down to hug Dog tight.

It wasn't Dog's fault that Puff had gotten chewed. It was his mother's fault, and Brody's fault—and most of all, Puff's fault, for existing in the first place. Mason had never liked Puff, anyway, and thought that nobody really did, except for Brody, and Mrs. Morengo, and the school secretary, and the principal, who were paid to like him. Nonetheless, it wasn't a pleasant thought that he would have to go into school tomorrow and tell everyone what had happened.

In his head he could hear the principal's voice during morning announcements: *It is my sad duty to*

inform you that three days before his scheduled appearance on television, Puff the Plainfield Dragon suffered a terrible misfortune. His head was eaten off by Mason Dixon's dog, Dog.

"What are we going to do?" Mason asked his mother.

She stood up straight, shoulders back, tummy tucked, as if ready to start singing "America!"

"I'm the one to blame for this, Mason. So I'm the one who's going to have to take care of it. I think I have a plan."

"What kind of plan?"

Her face had brightened. She obviously thought her plan was pretty terrific.

"Trust me on this one, Mason. I'm going to call Mrs. Morengo right now."

After supper—Pakistani lamb curry for his parents, a plain hamburger patty and plain green beans for Mason—Mason did some homework, trying hard not to think about Puff's demolition, Dog's disgrace, or his mother's conversation with Mrs. Morengo. His mom hadn't said anything about voice lessons to him during the meal, but a mysterious smile had played ominously around the corners of her mouth.

He finished writing the full draft of his story. The music teacher in the story, whom he was calling Mrs. Borengo, signaled to the piano-playing parent, Mr. Biffith, to begin the opening chords of the first song of the concert. It had taken a while for Mason to come up with the song for Pedro to refuse to play, but he finally settled on "You're a Grand Old Flag."

> Mr. Biffith pressed the keys. No sound came out.
>
> Mr. Biffith pounded on the keys. Pedro refused to play.
>
> "Mrs. Borengo!" Mr. Biffith called. "The piano is broken!"
>
> But he didn't know that the piano wasn't broken, not at all. The piano could have played perfectly well if he had wanted to. But Pedro the piano didn't want to. And Pedro the piano wasn't going to.

The story would have been more satisfying if Pedro could have said this out loud to everybody and they would have finally understood. It was too bad that they had to think Pedro was just a junky, broken-down piano instead of a piano with a strong sense of his own dignity and the spirit to stand up for himself. But under the influence of Nora's realism, Mason had made Pedro a piano that didn't talk.

Finally, in the story, Mr. Biffith gave up and sadly walked away. The students sang their song a cappella, which means without accompaniment. It all turned out okay.

Then, at the end of the concert, the custodian wheeled Pedro away to a pleasant storage room where he could spend the rest of his days with a saxophone and a violin that also didn't like to play in front of other people. But sometimes, late at night, they did play, all by themselves. People walking by the school at midnight said the school was haunted, but nobody believed them.

In big letters at the bottom of the last page, Mason wrote: THE END.

At the start of Platters practice the next morning, Mrs. Morengo made an announcement.

"For our concert, we are going to have three of our fabulous fifth graders announce our songs. Todd, Ella, and Zia, I'd like each of you to come up to the microphone during the concert and read the short speech I've prepared for you."

Mason sent a silent prayer heavenward: *Thank you, God, that I am not a fifth grader!* Speaking into the microphone at a televised Platters concert would be infinitely worse than leading the Pledge of Allegiance during morning announcements. It would be worse than singing in the concert, too, and that was going to be bad enough.

If only Mason could catch Mrs. Morengo after practice and ask her about being stage crew. The concert was now just two days away.

The three fifth graders who had been selected looked pleased as Mrs. Morengo handed them each an index card. Mason sent up a second prayer of gratitude that this time, as a lowly fourth grader, he had been safe from such a hideous possibility.

"Aren't the fourth graders going to get to do anything?" Brody's friend Julio asked.

"Yes!" Mrs. Morengo beamed.

Mason's prayers had been sent too soon.

"I've decided that one fourth grader is going to be dressed in a special Puff costume! For our concert on television, we should have a *live* Puff mascot, instead of just a stuffed toy."

Mason had never before heard Puff referred to so dismissively, as "just a stuffed toy" rather than "our beloved Puff who inspires us all."

"Do we *have* a Puff costume?" Emma Averill asked.

"Yes!" Mrs. Morengo said. "Or we will, by tomorrow. One of our very talented Platters parent helpers is sewing it today. Mason Dixon's mother has offered to use her sewing skills to make a Puff costume for us!"

She paused, as if expecting the students to begin applauding. When they didn't, she started them off with a few brisk *clap-claps* of her own, and they joined in. Mason clapped, too, but his palms felt sweaty.

This must be his mother's brilliant plan. He didn't know if she had confessed to Mrs. Morengo her reason for suggesting it. Mason hadn't even told Brody yet what had happened to Puff; he couldn't bear it.

"Who's going to be the mascot?" another kid asked.

Mrs. Morengo's eyes swept over the assembled fourth graders as if searching for inspiration.

"I've decided that our Puff mascot will also sing

a 'Puff' solo. Puff will start us off by singing the first verse and chorus of 'Puff the Plainfield Dragon,' wearing that adorable Puff costume, and then the rest of us will join in."

She smiled at Mason.

The smile slashed at his already-pounding heart.

No.

This couldn't be happening.

Even though Mrs. Morengo had made such a big fuss about his lovely voice. Even though she had said that she wanted him to sing a solo at a Platters concert sometime.

All too well he could imagine yesterday's conversation between his mother and his teacher.

Oh, singing a solo would be so good for Mason! And yes, Mrs. Morengo, we will definitely contact that voice teacher you recommended!

No.

Mason could not sing a solo.

Wearing a costume.

On television.

Mason's prayer now was short and to the point:

No, no, no, no, no, no, no.

11

"It wasn't easy making the choice," Mrs. Morengo continued. "And if anybody is disappointed at not getting this opportunity, remember that you fourth graders will have many chances to shine over the next two years."

But not to shine on television.

The shiniest—that is to say, the worst—shining of all.

"I've decided that our Puff for this first concert of the year will be—"

Mason Dixon.

"Brody Baxter."

If Mason hadn't already been sitting down in his place on the second riser, he might have fallen down, fallen clear off the riser again, overcome by the tidal wave of relief that washed over him.

Brody turned around to flash a delighted grin at Mason, his face alight with joy. Brody had thought it was an honor just to carry Puff home to be mended (actually, to be eaten alive—but Brody hadn't known that at the time and still didn't know it). Now Brody was having conferred upon him the far greater honor of being Puff himself.

"So let's practice 'Puff' right now with Brody

starting us off on the first verse," Mrs. Morengo said.

Brody came forward from the risers and stood in front of the assembled Platters.

"For the concert, of course, you'll be singing into the microphone. And wearing your Puff costume. Mrs. Dixon is designing the costume so that the audience will still be able to see your smiling face. All right, Brody, let's give it a try."

Mr. Griffith began playing the introduction.

Brody began to sing, his voice strong and true, his face radiant: "Puff the Plainfield Dragon lives at our school!"

Maybe it was a good thing, after all, that Dog had chewed Puff's head off. Not good for Puff, naturally, but good for Brody.

At the end of practice, Mason felt so giddy with continued relief that he didn't even feel shy about walking up to Mrs. Morengo as she was conferring with another mom about the design for the printed concert program.

"Puff on the cover, of course," he heard Mrs. Morengo say.

"Where *is* Puff?" the mom asked, casting her gaze

around the music room. "I'd like to be able to use him as a model for my drawing."

Mason turned quickly to go, clapping his hand on his head as if he suddenly remembered something he had forgotten to do, someplace far away from where he was standing right now.

It was too late.

"Mason?" Mrs. Morengo turned to him. "Your mother got me so excited about this wonderful idea of a live Puff mascot that I forgot to ask her how Puff's mending was coming along. We really do need him back here tomorrow, if at all possible, and definitely in time for the concert. The Platters have never performed without our lucky Puff to cheer us on."

So his mother hadn't told Mrs. Morengo yet.

Mason wasn't going to be the one to tell her, either, that lucky Puff, beloved by all Plainfield schoolchildren for generations, was gone forever.

"It's coming along," he said desperately.

The *mending* had been coming along just fine. It was the *chewing* that had turned out to be the problem.

He thought he felt another coughing fit starting up.

"Mrs. Morengo, I have another idea." Mason hurried on with his speech. "During the big storm in the raindrop song? What if someone—like me—turned the lights on and off to be lightning?"

Mrs. Morengo's wide face melted into the warmest smile that Mason had seen from her yet. "What a wonderful thought! I told you, Beth"—she said to the program-making mom—"my Platters never cease to astonish me."

"Can I be the person?" Mason pressed on. "To make the lightning?"

Mrs. Morengo hesitated. "Well, I suppose so, Mason, since it was your idea. But then you won't be up on the stage singing. And we'll miss hearing your lovely voice."

Correct.

"I thought I could also sort of be the stage crew for the whole show," Mason explained. "I could turn the gym lights off when the concert starts, and do the lightning, and then turn them on again when the concert's over. And—"

Mason tried to think of something else useful that he could do to justify not singing.

"And I could check if Pedro's piano bench—I

mean, if the piano bench—is in the right position. And if the microphones are the right height."

Mason was sorry he had suggested fiddling with the microphones. The last thing he wanted to do was to dash up on the stage and try to adjust the mikes, which probably wouldn't be working in the first place, as mikes never did at the crucial moment. Mason himself had never spoken into a microphone—or even touched one—in his life. The televised concert would be a bad time to start.

"Or maybe not the microphones," he corrected himself. "Just the lights. And the piano bench."

"But, Mason, I could have a parent helper do those things."

"Yes, but I'd really like to do it," Mason said. "It's been a dream of mine to be on a stage crew. And to do the lights for a big concert—that would just be so cool."

"All right," Mrs. Morengo agreed. "You may be our one-man Plainfield Platters stage crew!"

For the second time in less than an hour, Mason felt his knees go weak with relief.

Nothing could go wrong just turning the gym

lights off, then on-and-off-and-on-and-off, and then on again when the concert ended.

Could it?

"Which do you think is grander," Brody asked Mason as they hung their backpacks on the coat rack at the back of Coach Joe's room. Brody had waited for Mason outside the music room door while he had his conversation with Mrs. Morengo. "To be a royal can opener in the king and queen's palace, or to sing on television?"

Mason would hate both; probably he'd hate the singing more. But he knew what answer he was supposed to give. "Singing on television."

"That's what I think, too."

Nora came up behind them. "Congratulations, Brody!" she said.

In a low voice, as Brody raced over to tell Coach Joe his big news, Nora asked Mason, "What happened to the other Puff?"

"What makes you think something happened to him?"

It wasn't that Mason didn't want to tell her—he

knew Nora could be trusted with a secret—but he was curious about how she had guessed. Nora Alpers: scientist, bridge builder, detective.

"It just seems strange. You take Puff—stuffed Puff—home to mend him for the concert, and then all of a sudden he isn't even going to be in the concert."

In an even lower voice, Mason whispered one word to Nora: "Dog."

"Oh, no," Nora said.

"Oh, yes," said Mason.

And stuffed Puff was still supposed to be in the concert, or at least there at the concert, and he didn't exist anymore.

To change the subject, in case anyone else came into earshot, Mason told Nora, "Mrs. Morengo said I can be the stage crew. So that was a great idea."

"Cool."

"And I finished my story last night. Pedro does go on strike, and he never has to play in public for anyone ever again. I think it turned out pretty good. It's not really great, like Dunk's story, or anything, but it turned out okay."

"Dunk's story—" Nora started to say something about Dunk's story, but then the second bell rang, and it was time to salute the flag.

That morning, Coach Joe's class had art down in the art room. They were working on pointillist paintings, in the style of the French impressionist painter Georges Seurat: paintings that were made up entirely of little tiny dots. From a distance, the dots all merged together, so they didn't look like dots anymore, but close up you could see the whole picture was nothing but dots, dots, dots. So the goal was to make a picture out of dots that didn't look as if it was made out of dots.

Mason wondered what the point of this particular painting technique was supposed to be, but he kept his thoughts about it to himself.

Brody's dots had been neat and orderly, but today his dots were becoming wild and carefree, splashed down on his paper any which way. He was humming "Puff the Plainfield Dragon" as he painted. Mason could tell it was all Brody could do to keep on painting rows of dots instead of flinging down his brush and hugging himself with joy.

Then a shadow passed over Brody's face, and he did lay down his brush for a minute.

"Mason?"

"What?"

"Mason, you don't mind that she picked me, do you?"

"Of course not!"

"Instead of you? I mean, she said you were the one who should have a solo sometime. And you're the one whose mother is making the costume. So if you did mind—" Mason saw Brody swallowing hard. "I could tell her that I don't want to do it, and that she should pick you instead."

"Brody!" Mason didn't know if he wanted to hug Brody or shake him. "I. Don't. Like. To. Sing. Remember?"

"Are you sure?"

"Y-E-S."

Happy again, Brody picked up his brush and began painting more bright and sloppy dots, bouncy and springy dots practically dancing off the paper.

Sitting nearby, Nora was working on her painting with precision. Nora's dots could have been printed by a machine.

She started to say something, then stopped, and then finally said, "Did either of you think Dunk's new, longer Footie story sounded too good to be written by Dunk?"

Mason and Brody exchanged glances.

"It *was* good," Mason said. "But Dunk does like sports. Especially football."

In third grade, Dunk had thrown a football at Brody's head with remarkably perfect aim.

"Dunk didn't write that story," Nora said. "He copied it off the Internet."

"There's a story about Footie the football on the *Internet*?" Brody asked.

A yellow dot of paint was on the end of Brody's nose now, as if the bright, golden joy inside him was seeping out through his skin.

"No, silly," Nora said. She gave Brody's arm a

whack of friendly impatience. "He stuck Footie's name in whenever the real story said 'football.' But all the other stuff about the game—the intercepted pass by the receiver at the thirty-seven-yard line, blah, blah, blah—Dunk copied."

"Are you going to tell Coach Joe?" Mason asked.

"He's going to know, anyway. I mean, it's pretty obvious."

Obvious to Nora.

Just the way that Puff's calamity had been obvious to Nora.

The calamity that would all too soon be obvious to the entire heartbroken school.

"I think I might tell Dunk," Nora said. "That I know."

Mason wasn't sure whether he wanted her to alert Dunk or not. It would be satisfying to see Dunk get in trouble. At art camp last summer, Dunk had ruined practically every single artwork of Brody's, and yet he had never gotten in trouble. When Dunk's big bad dog, Wolf, had attacked Dog, Dunk hadn't gotten in trouble.

Dunk *had* said he was sorry that time. Mason had

to admit that Dunk had looked extremely sorry, too. But Dunk had deserved to be sorry.

And if Dunk had copied his story, he deserved to get in trouble and be sorry about that, too.

Now there was a yellow dot on Brody's chin, and one on his left cheek. Brody was turning into his own pointillist painting of a very happy boy.

Mason looked across the room at Dunk, who was busy flicking drops of paint onto the arm of poor Sheng, who was stuck sitting next to him and was obviously too afraid of Dunk to say anything about it.

Yes, it would be very satisfying if, for once, Dunk got into trouble. Big trouble.

12

"So, Mom," Mason said as he sat down at the kitchen table after school with his three Fig Newtons and a glass of milk. "Mrs. Morengo asked me about the real Puff. She said he needs to be at school tomorrow, because a mom is drawing his picture for the concert program. And the Platters have never performed without Puff to cheer them on. What are we going to do?"

Dog lay at Mason's feet, contentedly chewing a rawhide bone. Mason's mom had called the vet after the Puff disaster for advice on what to do about Dog's chewing. The vet said to give Dog lots of extra chewing opportunities so he could channel his chewing energies more appropriately. Mason's dad had been right all along.

Mason's mother gave him another mysterious smile. Mason had learned once in art class that a smile like that was called a Mona Lisa smile, after the expression on a famous portrait painted by the Italian artist Leonardo da Vinci. But Mason wasn't in the mood for a Mona Lisa smile right now.

"Tell me!" he pleaded.

"I will in a minute. But first tell me: was Brody thrilled with his solo?"

Mason stared at her. "How did you know she was going to give the solo to Brody?"

"Mrs. Morengo told me yesterday, when we were talking on the phone. And who else could be Puff, if not Brody? He's such a cute size, with that great big personality—"

Mason's face must have given him away.

"Mason, you didn't think—"

Was she also going to accuse him of having wanted to be Puff? She couldn't, not his own mother. It was bad enough coming from his best friend, but at least Brody's excuse was that he honestly couldn't imagine that anybody in the universe might not want to be Puff.

She reached over and smoothed his hair, not that

it needed smoothing. "Oh, honey, I should have told you, so you wouldn't worry. I just thought it would be such a great surprise."

Apparently she had forgotten that Mason hated surprises. At least she had remembered that Mason hated singing.

"But, honey, Mrs. Morengo did say that you're doing so well in the Platters! And, can you believe it, she even said that we should consider getting you voice lessons!"

The doorbell rang. Dog abandoned his bone and jumped up to go help answer it.

"Speaking of surprises . . . ," his mother said as she exited the kitchen behind Dog.

She returned carrying an enormous cardboard carton, practically as big as Brody.

"Dog, sit!" Mason's mom commanded. Dog sat.

"Dog, bone!" she commanded. Dog resumed his contented chewing.

Using a kitchen knife, Mason's mom slit open the tape sealing the top flaps of the box. Then, to Mason's great astonishment, she lifted out a large stuffed animal. A large stuffed dragon. A faded, oversized stuffed dragon that looked exactly like Puff.

It *was* Puff. But how could that be?

"I found another Puff on eBay! You have no idea how relieved I was when I found it and they said they could overnight it to me. I came up with the live-mascot idea just in case Puff didn't get here in time for the concert. And it turned out to be the perfect idea, didn't it?"

Mason couldn't decide if he should feel enormously relieved for the third time that day—he did feel enormously relieved—or sad for the first Puff, gone forever, and now replaced by this look-alike copy. Everyone at Plainfield Elementary—from Mrs. Miller on down to the littlest kindergartners—would think this was the true lucky Puff who had served Plainfield Elementary faithfully for twenty years.

Everyone except for Mason. And Nora.

Another thought struck him. Was this *cheating*? Like Dunk's copying of his Footie story?

"Are you ever going to tell Mrs. Morengo what really happened?" Mason asked her.

She paused, as if asking herself the same question. "You know, I think we should just file this one under the heading 'all's well that ends well.'"

She was probably right.

He hoped that in another two days he'd be able to file his first—and last?—Platters concert under that same heading.

"I'm going right now to put Puff the Second up in my office, behind closed doors," she said, even though Dog seemed much less interested in Puff the Second than he'd been in Puff the First. Maybe Puff's head hadn't been that tasty—or easy to digest—after all. Or maybe he was cured of chewing stuffed animals for good.

Mason's mother bustled away with Puff in her arms.

While she was gone, Mason pondered a question of his own: should he tell her he was going to be the stage crew for the show, or leave it as a surprise, since she was the one who liked surprises?

He voted for the surprise. He hoped she'd think it was a good surprise. As Nora had said, he'd still be in the concert. Well, sort of in the concert.

He'd still be giving the Plainfield Platters a fair try. Well, sort of a fair try.

But he wouldn't be using his lovely voice, the voice that his teacher had praised, the voice that was worthy of voice lessons. He wouldn't be standing up on the stage with Brody and the other Platters, singing with all his might about Puff, as his father filmed every second of the concert with his camcorder and his mother wiped proud tears from her eyes.

Oh, if only he could file the Plainfield Platters forever under "done, done, done."

★ ★ ★

Brody wore his Puff costume for the Platters practice held the next morning, Thursday morning, on the stage in the gym. Mason's mom had tried it on him the night before and made a few last-minute adjustments so it would fit him perfectly.

The Thursday-morning practice was also Mason's first time working as stage crew. Oh, the bliss of not being on those risers with the other singers! He thought he did a good job as lightning guy. It would be a much cooler special effect tomorrow evening, when the gym would be dark, rather than bright with the morning sunlight that was now streaming through the high windows.

Mason caught Dunk staring at him, and sure enough, Dunk came up to Mason and Brody as soon as the practice was over.

"Did Morengo kick you out?" he asked hopefully, walking beside them as they headed to class.

Brody answered indignantly. "No! If she was going to kick out anybody, it would be *you*."

"Well, why aren't you singing anymore, like a dumb lady opera singer? Why are you just turning the stupid lights on and off for two seconds?"

"I'm the stage crew," Mason said with what he hoped sounded like quiet dignity.

Dunk guffawed. "Was that your idea or her idea?"

It had been Nora's idea, actually, but Mason refused to answer.

"Either it was Morengo's idea because she finally realized you stink so bad she didn't want you to ruin the concert for everybody else. Or it was your idea because you're a scaredy-cat."

Mason tried to keep his face from betraying any emotion, but he could tell that Dunk knew he had guessed correctly.

"You're a little scaredy teapot, short and stout," Dunk chortled.

"He is not!" Brody almost yelled. "The stage crew is a very important part of a show. It's the most important part!"

"It's definitely more important than singing a dumb solo in a dumb costume like a dumb Puff baby," Dunk agreed.

Mason knew it was his turn now to defend Brody, but he couldn't think of anything stinging enough to say.

Nora had been walking behind them, evidently listening all the time. Now she caught up to them, her eyes flashing. But her voice, as always, was calm and steady.

"I found an interesting site on the Internet last night," she said to the three of them, as if simply offering a tidbit of neutral information. "It had a very detailed description of last year's Super Bowl game. You'd like it, Dunk, since you're so interested in football. You know, because of your story about Footie."

That was all she said. But it was enough to make Dunk flush a deep, dull red.

"Oh, and I made a printout of it," Nora added

casually. "I thought Coach Joe might like it, too. Since he loves sports so much. Except, of course, when anybody is cheating."

She gave Dunk a last friendly smile.

Mason didn't turn to look again at Dunk as they stashed their backpacks and took their seats in Coach Joe's classroom.

Dunk ripped up his story. Mason saw him doing it. Not that Dunk ever did anything quietly.

Rip! Rip! Dunk tore the paper he had already torn, again and again, until his desk was littered with a heap of paper scraps, some of them falling onto the floor as well.

The sound was loud enough that Coach Joe looked up from his desk. "Hey, Dunk," he said in his cheerful tone of voice, "what's up?"

Dunk looked close to tears. "I ripped up 'Footie.'" He turned to glare at Nora, as if to say, *See what you made me do?*

"Whoa," Coach Joe said softly. He formed his hand into a time-out T. "Dunk, how about our own private huddle, one on one?" He nodded his head toward the hall.

Dunk stayed in his seat, obviously past caring if anyone else heard what he had to say.

"My story stinks! Sheng said so!"

Coach Joe looked expectantly at Sheng.

"I didn't say it stank. I said it was short. That's all I said."

"You said it was *too* short. And I tried to make it longer, but I couldn't think of stuff to write, so I copied some stuff from Wikipedia, and she"—he gave a baleful jerk of his head toward Nora—"printed it out and was going to give it to you, so now I've ripped it up, and I'll get a zero, and my dad will freak out, and he won't let me play football, and it's all her fault!"

Dunk's cheeks were red, and his lower lip stuck out, quivering. His eyes were bright with tears; he rubbed them defiantly as he glared again at Nora.

"Whoa," Coach Joe said a second time, even more softly, as if trying to figure out how his team could have fallen apart so badly so close to the start of the season.

Mason sneaked a glance at Nora. She didn't seem upset that Dunk blamed her for his ripped-up story. It was as if she had just poked a stick into an ant tunnel and was watching with calm curiosity for what the ants would do next.

There was a long silence, Dunk sniffling and Coach Joe obviously thinking about how to get his team back on the field.

"Well, Dunk," Coach Joe finally said, "if you copied your story from the Internet, you did the right thing in throwing it away. It's better to lose the game than to win it by not playing fair and square. Copying somebody else's work, and then trying to pass it off as your own, is plagiarism, and it's wrong, no two ways about it."

Coach Joe went on. "Now, the story is due tomorrow. As far as I can see, you have two options. Write your own Footie story, short or long, telling Footie's story as *you* want to tell it. But maybe the problem is that you weren't all that interested in Footie in the first place, and you really wanted to write about someone else. Your friend the toilet."

A couple of kids giggled, not in a mean way, but just because they couldn't help it. Even Dunk's mouth twisted into a shaky grin.

"You said your dad didn't want you to write about

the toilet. Maybe your dad didn't know that on Coach Joe's team, any subject is A-okay. Because you know what the first rule of writing is for my class?"

Mason tried to guess, but couldn't.

"*Have fun*. If the writer is having fun writing, the reader will probably have fun reading. So maybe it's goodbye, Footie the football, and hello, Tommy the toilet. Or maybe you want to give Footie one more chance—*your* best shot. Either way, it's up to you."

Coach Joe sat back down behind his desk. "So that's my locker-room pep talk, team."

The next time Mason looked over at Dunk, Dunk's hand was racing furiously across the page and Dunk was grinning to himself as he wrote a line he seemed to think was particularly hilarious. Mason had a feeling that Tommy the toilet was busy flushing something very interesting.

13

That night, the night before the concert, Mason and his mother finished reading *Ballet Shoes*. The book ended with Pauline going off to Hollywood to be a movie star, Posy going off to Czechoslovakia to be a ballerina, and Petrova going off to fly planes with "Gum," their great-uncle Matthew. It was a completely satisfying ending.

Dog thought so, too. He gave a low whimper of appreciation when Mason's mother shut the book after the last page.

"If you liked *Ballet Shoes*," she told Mason, "there's a whole series of Shoes books. *Theatre Shoes*, *Dancing Shoes*, *Movie Shoes*, *Skating Shoes*, *Tennis Shoes*, *Circus Shoes*. All kinds of shoes."

"Do they all have shoes in them?"

"No, they're all about talented children following their dreams."

"Are any of them about ordinary, nontalented children who don't have any dreams?" Mason hadn't meant for his question to come out sounding so bitter.

"Oh, Mason, you're only in fourth grade. There's still plenty of time for you to find your talents and your dreams. Anyway, there's Jane in *Movie Shoes*. Her talent is loving her dog. Really."

"Then why is it called *Movie Shoes* and not *Dog Shoes?*"

"Because Jane does end up being in a movie. She plays the part of Mary in a movie version of *The Secret Garden*. But what she really loves is spending time with her dog, Chewing Gum."

That was a strange name for a dog, in Mason's opinion. But he guessed all dogs couldn't be named Dog.

His mother kissed Mason goodnight and dropped a kiss on Dog's head, too.

"Get a good night's sleep. Tomorrow's your big day!" she said as she turned off Mason's light and closed the door.

Mason wished she hadn't said it.

★ ★ ★

Mason was surprised, at the dress rehearsal before school on Friday morning, to find that the Platters were only part of the Beulah Brighton Belvedere School for the Arts celebration concert. First the fifth-grade handbell choir performed, and then some kid—a third grader!—played a showy piece on his violin, and a group of girls did Irish step dancing. The Platters performed last, beginning with "America!" and then "Summer Storm," and finishing, of course, with "Puff the Plainfield Dragon."

The Platters' portion of the rehearsal was a disaster, from start to finish. It took forever for the singers to find their places on the risers, even though they'd sung on risers every day that week. Four letters were upside down in the finale of "America!" One kid came in too soon for the first "Drip, drop" of the raindrop song. The mike didn't work for Brody's solo.

Worst of all, Mason was so fascinated by the spectacle of all these mistakes and mishaps that, standing at the light switches by the side door of the gym, he forgot to flash the lightning until the storm was almost over. Not that anyone could see the flashing lights in broad daylight. But he knew he had failed miserably.

Mrs. Morengo tried to be encouraging. "Now, Platters, you know what they say in the world of theater, don't you? The worse the dress rehearsal, the better the show!"

Mason was sure that saying had been invented only to give false hope after terrible dress rehearsals.

"I would be worried if the dress rehearsal *hadn't* been like this," Mrs. Morengo insisted.

A lie if Mason had ever heard one.

All day, Coach Joe's students were unable to settle down to division, Native Americans, the life cycle of a crayfish. Finally he gave up and took them outside for extra recess.

Mason, Brody, and Nora found a cool spot at the edge of the blacktop, sitting at a picnic table under an enormous oak tree.

"Are you nervous?" Nora asked Brody.

"No!" Brody appeared shocked by the question. "We've been singing 'Puff' since kindergarten! And if the mike doesn't work, I'll just belt it out."

He stood up on top of the picnic table, as if preparing to demonstrate his show-stopping technique.

"That's okay," Nora said. "We believe you."

"Plus, no one else will have seen my costume yet, so think how amazed they'll be."

The plan was for Brody to slip off the risers during the applause following the raindrop song—assuming that there was any applause—and dart offstage to zip into his costume, while the last fifth-grade speaker announced the final number of the program.

Mason hoped the zipper didn't get stuck.

Or break.

He knew he shouldn't be thinking things like that.

But he always did.

"When they see me?" Brody continued. "When the audience sees me? They're going to go like this: *Awwwwww.*"

He imitated the audience again, their long, slow sigh of awestruck appreciation at his outstanding cuteness: "*Awwwwwwww.*"

Nora swatted him, and Brody sat down next to Mason on the picnic bench, his eyes still shining from his anticipated glory.

Mason hoped Dunk didn't push anyone off the risers during the concert, though at least this time it wouldn't be him.

He hoped the piano didn't break right in the middle of a song—that Pedro would decide to wait a little longer before going on strike and refusing to play.

He hoped all the letters for "America!" would be right side up.

He hoped he remembered to flash the lights.

Most of all, he hoped his mother would think it was okay that he was flashing the lights instead of singing with his voice-lesson voice.

He knew he shouldn't be thinking things like that.

But he always did.

★ ★ ★

The students were supposed to be at school at 6:15; the concert was set to begin at seven o'clock. There was really no reason why they all had to arrive forty-five minutes early. Mason figured the early time was Mrs. Morengo's way of making sure that even her straggler Platters wouldn't be late.

Even though he wasn't going to be singing with the others, Mason wore his Platters T-shirt, the one that had originally been Brody's, before they traded shirts. So his parents still had no clue about the stage-crew surprise.

The gym was packed, each folding chair occupied by a proud parent, a squirming sibling, or even a teacher. At his post by the light switches, Mason saw Coach Joe, who gave him a big thumbs-up, and Mrs. Prindle, who shook her head warningly at him for no reason at all. In the back of the gym, the cameraman from Channel 9 News was staggering under the weight of the largest camera Mason had ever seen.

Mrs. Morengo gave Mason a signal. He flipped the three switches for the lights that lit up the seating area in the gym, leaving only the lights shining upon the stage.

So far, so good.

Mrs. Miller came out, to loud applause from the audience. She made a speech that went on too long about the great honor for Plainfield Elementary of being named a Beulah Brighton Belvedere School for the Arts. Mason still had no idea who Beulah Brighton Belvedere was or why she liked the arts so much.

The handbells chimed, and the violin prodigy played his violin, and the Irish dancers danced.

Mason could see the Platters standing in line in the wings, waiting for their moment to take the stage. Part of Mason thought it would be better to go first and get it over with. On the other hand, if you were last, there was always some chance of an earthquake or a tornado that would keep you from having to perform at all.

"And now," Mrs. Miller said into her microphone, "last but certainly not least, our beloved Plainfield PLATTERS!"

The audience cheered as the Platters marched in formation up onto the stage.

Mason felt a teensy-weensy pang that he wasn't with them. He knew his parents would be craning their necks for a first glimpse of him there on the risers and wondering why they couldn't see him anywhere.

He concentrated on gathering his strength for his big moment as lightning guy. And hoping that the "America!" letters would all be right side up this time.

And they were! The first number was definitely fine, even better than fine. Maybe that old saying about the bad dress rehearsal wasn't bogus, after all.

The raindrop song, too, was more impressive than Mason had expected.

Bang, crash came the drums and cymbals.

Flash, flash went the lights. *Mason's* lights.

He thought he could hear the audience give a small gasp of astonishment at the cleverness of this special effect. But, with all eyes on the stage, nobody—including his parents—would know that he was the one doing it.

The storm subsided.

"Drip. Drop. Drip."

"Drip."

"Drip."

A moment of silence—would there be one last raindrop? No. Mrs. Morengo turned to face the audience, so they would know the song was over and it was time to applaud. And they did.

As Mason watched, Brody disappeared from the risers to put on his costume. Zia read her little speech from Mrs. Morengo's index card:

"Our last song is dear to the hearts of all Plainfield Elementary students, parents, teachers, and staff. For twenty years, we have been singing about our love for our wonderful mascot, who inspires us to be our best every day in every way. Ladies and gentlemen, as our final number for this special evening, we give you 'Puff the Plainfield Dragon'!"

A small green dragon walked slowly to the middle of the stage.

"Awwwwwww!" went the audience.

Mason could see Brody's face poking through the face hole in his costume. Brody wasn't smiling. Perhaps he had decided that Puff should have a more solemn expression, as befitted his sacred status as Plainfield Elementary's tradition and treasure.

Mr. Griffith began to play.

Brody did not begin to sing.

Mr. Griffith smiled up encouragingly at Brody and kept the introduction going for a bit longer.

Puff the Plainfield Dragon stood silent, voiceless, motionless—paralyzed, Mason could see, by complete and utter terror.

14

Sing, Brody! Mason willed with every fiber of his being. *Sing!*

Brody continued to stand there, stock still, no sound whatsoever coming out of his mouth. He looked as if any second his face would crumple into tears and he would be crying in front of hundreds of people in the Plainfield Elementary gymnasium and tens of thousands more watching on TV.

Mrs. Morengo wasn't facing the audience, so Mason could see the pleading expression on her face, and he could see her arms raised imploringly toward Brody. *Sing, Brody!*

Somebody had to start singing—Brody, all the assembled Platters, or somebody else. If a few more seconds went by without any sounds coming out of

anybody's mouth, Brody would be known forever as the failed Puff at the most disastrous concert in Platters history.

Sing, somebody!

And then, to the amazement of Mason himself, *he* was that somebody.

More nimbly than he could have imagined, Mason walked out onto the stage and joined Brody at the mike.

Mr. Griffith came around again to the familiar opening cue, and Mason opened his mouth to prepare to sing, praying that this time he wouldn't have a spasm of coughing. After all, if there was one song on this earth that he could sing, this was it.

"Puff the Plainfield Dragon," Mason sang.

Brody joined in. "Lives at our school."

"Puff helps us to do our work and follow every rule," the two friends sang together. Brody's voice was loud and confident now.

"Puff is loved by everyone because he is so cool! Every day we shout hooray that Puff lives at our school! Oh. . . ."

The Plainfield Platters added their voices to the next chorus. Mason couldn't see them, but he knew

that standing behind him on the risers, Nora and Dunk, Sheng, Julio, Alastair, and Bradley were all singing, too. Brody was belting out the song with all his big Brody heart, his face shining once again in its usual Brodyish way, as if it had been buttered with happiness.

Although they hadn't rehearsed it like this, Mrs. Morengo turned toward the audience and invited them to sing along. The gymnasium swelled with the sound. Mason wondered if even Mrs. Prindle and the Channel 9 cameraman would be able to resist taking part.

"Puff the Plainfield Dragon!" Mason sang to the

brand-new but still lucky stuffed dragon propped up against the side of the stage.

"Every day we shout hooray that Puff lives at our school!"

"Oh, Mason, we were so worried!" his mother said as she crushed him into a hug once the concert was over and kids were meeting their parents in the hallway outside the gym. "We looked and looked and couldn't find you anywhere! But then—oh, Mason, you didn't tell us that *you* were going to have a solo, along with Brody!"

Mason's dad stopped fiddling with his camcorder and joined in the hug.

Mason didn't know how much to tell them. So all he said was, hoping it didn't sound too much like bragging, "The lightning during the raindrop song? That was me, too."

"Oh, Mason!" his mother said, seemingly overcome by the thought of his solo *plus* his extremely clever lighting effect.

"And, Dan, what do you think about voice lessons? Mason, should we call that woman Mrs. Morengo suggested? Would you like us to do that?"

"Um, that would be a no," Mason said.

His mother exchanged a glance with his father but didn't say anything more, distracted by the compliments and congratulations from other parents crowding up to them.

"The two of you looked so cute together!" Brody's mother said, busy hugging Mason as Mason's mother was busy hugging Brody.

Nora flashed him a huge smile. Even Dunk's parents said something nice while Dunk stood staring down at the floor.

Maybe Mason should ask Coach Joe on Monday if he could revise his Pedro story. He thought maybe Pedro was ready now to come out of retirement and play again, taking his place up on the stage, in the spotlight, making music for all to hear.

Anything was possible.

ACKNOWLEDGMENTS

It is such a pleasure to be able to thank some of the wonderful, brilliant, creative people who helped bring this book into being: my longtime Boulder writing group (Marie DesJardin, Mary Peace Finley, Ann Whitehead Nagda, Leslie O'Kane, Phyllis Perry, and Elizabeth Wrenn); my unfailingly insightful and encouraging editor, Nancy Hinkel; my wise and caring agent, Stephen Fraser; consistently helpful Jeremy Medina; magnificently sharp-eyed copy editors Janet Frick and Artie Bennett; Guy Francis for his funny, tender pictures; and Isabel Warren-Lynch and Sarah Hokanson for their appealing book design. And one huge thank-you goes to Jennifer Teets, who invited me to give an author talk several years ago at Platteville Elementary School in Platteville, Colorado. Their school song, "Puff the Platteville Dragon," became the inspiration for Mason's school song here.

CLAUDIA MILLS is the author of over forty books for young readers. She loves to sing, loudly, in front of large audiences, but unfortunately nobody else ever wants her to do this. So instead she curls up with her cat, Snickers, on her couch at home in Boulder, Colorado, drinking hot chocolate and writing. Visit Claudia at claudiamillsauthor.com.

Don't miss

next big ~~disaster~~ adventure!

Here's a sneak peek at:

Mason Dixon: Basketball Disasters by Claudia Mills

Available January 2012 from Alfred A. Knopf Books for Young Readers

Excerpt from *Mason Dixon: Basketball Disasters* by Claudia Mills

Published in the United States by Alfred A. Knopf Books for Young Readers,
an imprint of Random House Children's Books, a division of Random House, Inc., New York.

1

On the Plainfield Elementary School playground, Mason Dixon watched from a safe distance as his best friend, Brody Baxter, aimed his basketball at the hoop.

At least Mason had thought it was a safe distance.

The ball struck the front of the rim and shot back directly toward Mason's head.

"Watch out!" Brody shouted.

Mason watched, but didn't exactly watch *out*. Instead, he stared with horrified fascination as the ball zoomed toward him. Then, a split second before it would have knocked him to the blacktop—"Fourth-Grade Boy Killed on Basketball Court"—he made a saving catch.

Mason's golden retriever—named Dog, short

for Dog of Greatness—gave an appreciative bark as Mason tossed the basketball back to Brody. Then Dog gave another appreciative bark as Brody caught it. Dog lived at Mason's house, because Brody's dad was desperately allergic to all furry pets, but both boys shared Dog and loved him equally.

"Hey, Mason," Brody said, practically dancing as he dribbled in place beneath the hoop. "You're good! You have quick reflexes!"

Well, yes, sometimes a person's reflexes became surprisingly good when the person was facing impending death-by-basketball.

"Come on, Mason, shoot some with me. Dog, you can come and shoot some, too."

Dog wagged his tail at the sound of his name. Besides, Dog loved playing with a ball, any ball. Despite having only three legs, Dog thought that retrieving balls, or sticks—or any tossed object—was life's greatest joy.

This was one way in which Mason and Dog were different.

"Did I tell you I talked to my parents?" Brody asked. "I told them I want to try basketball at the YMCA for a season."

Mason would have guessed this without Brody telling him anything. Of course Brody would want to try basketball. Brody was interested in trying everything. He was finishing up a short soccer season right now; he'd play baseball in the spring. Why not play basketball, too?

That was one way in which Mason and Brody were different.

It was almost evening, on a mid-October Friday, and the Plainfield Elementary playground was deserted, except for Mason, Brody, and Dog. Neither boy had a basketball hoop on his garage, so this was the perfect place for playing basketball.

If any place was a perfect place for playing basketball.

Mason edged slowly onto the court. Brody took a few more dribbles and then shot again, and missed again.

"Get the rebound!" Brody called to Mason.

Mason managed to stumble after the ball and grab it before it rolled off into the long grass at the edge of the blacktop. He knew the basic idea of how to play basketball, from playing it for a few weeks each year in P.E., but he had never been good at it, or good at any sport, for that matter.

"Now shoot!"

Without bothering to take careful aim, Mason tossed the ball in the general direction of the hoop.

"You're not even trying," Brody scolded. He tossed the ball back to Mason.

This time Mason studied the distance to the hoop before releasing the ball. His eyes widened with disbelief as, without even grazing the rim, the ball sailed neatly through the hoop and into Brody's waiting hands.

Brody cheered. Mason continued to stare at the hoop.

"Besides, you're tall," Brody said as he hugged the ball to his chest. "You'd be good at basketball because you're tall."

People often said that to Mason, that he'd be good at basketball because he was tall. They seemed to be forgetting that basketball involved a few other things besides height, such as skill in shooting, passing, dribbling, and guarding. Little things like that.

"I know I'm short," Brody said as he began

dribbling the ball in slow circles around Mason, "but that can be an advantage in basketball."

Mason didn't say it, but he couldn't help thinking: *Then why are so many professional basketball players seven feet tall?*

"A short guy can dart in and out, and the tall guys won't even know what's coming at them."

Brody assumed a crouching position, as if to block an opponent's shot.

"But you know the real reason why I'm going to be good at basketball?" Brody asked Mason.

Mason knew Brody wasn't really bragging. Brody was just so in love with the idea of playing basketball for the first time, and being good at it, *great* at it, that his enthusiasm bubbled out of him like happy steam from a singing teakettle.

"Why?" Mason asked, because Brody was clearly expecting him to.

"Because I have *hustle*," Brody said. "I do. I have hustle."

Something Mason decidedly didn't have. And never would have.

"Look," Brody said as he shot again. This time the ball teetered on the rim and then dropped in. "If you sign up for the team with me, then I'll have a ride to all the practices and the games."

"What about your parents? Why can't they drive you?"

"They told me I'm already doing too many sports this year, and Cammie and Cara are playing basketball, too, and it's their only sport this year, and so they get priority. That's what they said."

Mason let Brody bounce-pass the ball to him, and he took another shot. This time he felt a strange satisfaction in missing, as if his wide shot proved Brody wrong about Mason's supposedly great potential as a tall player with quick reflexes.

"Um, Brody?" Mason apparently needed to remind him. "I'm not what you would call a sports person."

"That's like what you said when we got Dog, remember? That you weren't a pet person? And now you love Dog."

Mason tried to hide his scowl. He hated being reminded that he had agreed to adopt Dog a few months ago only because of Brody's begging and pleading.

"And then you said you didn't want to be in the Plainfield Platters, remember? You said you weren't a singing person?"

The Platters were the fourth- and fifth-grade choir at Mason and Brody's school. Mason had joined it this year, against his will, and he had to admit that it hadn't been terrible so far. He and Brody had even sung a solo together at the last concert.

Brody went on. "Mason, I really think my parents mean it this time, that I have too many activities and they're not going to drive me to this one."

Mason cast about for another way Brody could get his rides. "Does Sheng want to play basketball? Or Julio? Or Alastair?"

Sheng was Brody's second-best friend. Julio was Brody's third-best friend. Alastair was Brody's fourth-best friend.

Brody shook his head at each name. "Either they're already on another team, or they don't want to play basketball."

"But I don't want to play basketball, either!"

Somehow Mason had already lost the battle.

"Believe me," Brody said happily, "this is going to be great!"

Mason sighed.